Other Books by Patricia Taylor Wells

The Eyes of the Doe
Kaleidoscope
LodeStar
Mademoiselle Renoir à Paris
Maple Point
The Sand Rose

Carousel

PATRICIA TAYLOR WELLS

Carousel

SHORT STORIES & MUSINGS

GusGus Press • Bedazzled Ink Publishing
Fairfield, California

978-1-960373-58-8 paperback

Cover Design
by

Sapling
Studio

GusGus Press
a division of
Bedazzled Ink Publishing Company
Fairfield, California
http://www.bedazzledink.com

"Before there were novels, there were short stories passed down orally among members of a tribe, making them the oldest form of education. These stories have helped preserve cultural beliefs, traditions, and history for thousands of generations. As children, we learned valuable life lessons, especially about good and evil, through fairy tales, fables, myths, and Biblical stories such as the parables of Jesus. As ancient as many of these stories are, they still have relevance in today's world.

"The modern short story, developed in nineteenth-century America, seeks more to entertain than to instruct. Among the most popular short story authors are Edgar Allan Poe, Oscar Wilde, O. Henry, Mark Twain, William Faulkner, and Ernest Hemingway."

—excerpt published in *Tyler Today Magazine*'s
"Authors Among Us" column, June/July 2020 issue,
by Patricia Taylor Wells

Among the Thorns

I stood there like a statue—frozen in place, unable to speak or even blink my eyes. It was almost dark. We talked outside the restaurant where we had met that evening for nearly an hour. The lights in the parking lot flashed across the rooftops of automobiles and onto the pavement, leaving Bryan's face in half-shadow. His eyes narrowed as he waited for me to continue. But there was nothing left to say. It was over. The eight long years we had been seeing each other were finally ending. I had thought the news about my job offer in Seattle would make Bryan realize he couldn't live without me. I should have known by the fact we had never moved in together that the commitment I had hoped for wasn't coming. Somehow, in the semi-darkness, I finally saw what a dead-end street I was on. And for the first time, I didn't feel the panic, the heartache, the emptiness that always washed over me each time I had thought about leaving him. I walked away without even looking back. I was proud of myself as I drove back to my lonely apartment.

I decided not to take the position in Seattle. In truth, I had not seriously considered it at all. I had used it as a pawn to get what I wanted from Bryan, but it had failed. If I stayed in Dallas, I would be surrounded by friends and could easily visit my family in Austin.

It was hard not having anyone special in my life. I kept busy with work and various activities designed to attract the young and single, like the wine pairing class at *La Fontaine's*, which met every Thursday evening for six weeks. Nothing was better than sampling good food and wine to soothe a broken heart.

Several tables were already filled when I arrived for my first class at the restaurant. I sat at an open spot across from two girls who were much younger than me. I noticed an attractive man, probably early thirties, sitting one table away from mine. After a moment or two, he got up and walked my way.

"Is anyone sitting here?" He gestured at the empty chair next to me.

"No, it's all yours," I said, barely looking up from the brochure with that evening's wine selections and small bites. I wasn't good at casual conversation.

Eventually, a younger guy joined the two girls. The three of them were soon deep in conversation. The guy sitting next to me made a few comments now and then, but mostly, we remained silent. I had never felt comfortable offering my opinion to those I didn't know well, even about something as benign as a glass of wine. When the class was over, the man extended his hand as he stood up to leave.

"I'm Bryan, by the way," he said. "Bryan Winters."

Just my luck—another Bryan.

"And I'm Lori Hunter." I shook his hand. "

"Do you ever go to the wine tastings at Pascal's?" Bryan asked.

" Occasionally," I lied. I don't know why I wanted to impress this man by pretending to be a regular at the trendiest wine bar in the city.

"Maybe I'll see you there sometime. Nice meeting you." Bryan turned and walked away before I could even respond.

He's not interested, I immediately concluded.

By the end of the fourth class, Bryan and I had become good friends. While walking out together after the session, he asked if I would like to have dinner with him over the weekend. I accepted, and on Saturday, we enjoyed a quiet, romantic evening at The Candlelight Inn. In the days and weeks that followed, we spent hours talking on the phone or texting. He made me laugh, and I felt comfortable being with him. From what I could tell, Bryan was a successful financial planner. Finally, a guy that had it all together. Everything about him looked promising.

As Thanksgiving came around, Bryan hinted that he had nowhere to go for the holidays. Although introducing him to my family felt too soon, I invited him to join me in Austin. He did, and from then on, our relationship grew to new heights. We both had plans to spend Christmas with our families: Bryan in Florida and me in Austin. But at least we would be together on New Year's Eve when we were scheduled to return to our jobs in Dallas. I was excited about how well things were moving along.

I arrived in Austin on the day before Christmas Eve. The next morning, I received a call from a coworker in my Dallas office.

"Hey, Lori," Allison greeted. "A beautiful bouquet of roses just arrived for you. What do you want me to do with them?"

"Roses?" I asked. "Who are they from?"

"Let me see," Allison said. "The card says *Love, Bryan*."

"I don't understand," I said. "Bryan knows I'm in Austin. Could you do me a favor and call the florist? There must be some mistake."

My heart quickened as I tried to figure things out. The roses must be from the other Bryan, I ventured. He's probably trying to get back together with me. Why would I have even thought of that? Was it possible I still had strong feelings for him? Strong enough to hope the flowers were from him rather than the new man in my life. Or maybe I just enjoyed the thought of him pining away for me.

Allison called me back after she spoke with the florist.

"Okay, there was a mistake," she explained. "The flowers were supposed to be delivered on New Year's Eve, not Christmas Eve."

"Well, then tell them to come pick up the flowers, but make sure they send me another bouquet on New Year's Eve." I hung up the phone and quickly shoved any thoughts about my former boyfriend into the back corners of my mind.

I decided not to tell Bryan about the mistake. I was sure now that his plans included much more than dinner and dancing when we saw each other again in Dallas. He was going to propose. I practically floated mid-air as I shared my news with my sister and mother. I knew the look on their faces. They felt like I was making too much out of a bouquet—that my expectations were sure to end in disappointment. I didn't care what they thought. I knew in my heart that Bryan wanted to marry me. I was thirty years old, and I was done wasting time on men who weren't ready to commit to a lasting relationship. My day had finally come, and I was soaring above the clouds.

I returned to work the following week on New Year's Eve. When my flowers arrived that morning, I was appalled. Some of the petals were faded and tired looking. I quickly determined they were the original roses the florist had mistakenly delivered on Christmas Eve.

After the roses were returned, they were put in the cooler to await redelivery a week later. I couldn't believe it. I wasn't about to let Bryan see them. I knew how important this day was for him.

I picked up the phone and called the florist, insisting they deliver fresh roses to me immediately.

Yes, I knew how busy they were on New Year's Eve, but it was their mistake to send the flowers on the wrong date, and then to deliver a worn-out bouquet on the intended date was unacceptable. Later that afternoon, a new vase of roses arrived at my office. One day, I thought, when Bryan and I were old and gray, we could sit back and laugh about this.

We started with dinner at The Candlelight Inn on New Year's Eve, where we had shared our first date. Next, we went to the rooftop club of a hotel, where we had gone several times for cocktails and dancing. It was one of our favorite spots. By the time we got there, the place was packed.

Bryan grew increasingly impatient as the hostess searched for our reservations on the long list before her.

"Last name Winters, you said?" the hostess looked up at Bryan.

"Yes, I called over a week before Christmas," Bryan replied.

"I'm sorry, sir. I don't have you on my list."

"I made reservations," Bryan insisted. "This is your mistake, not mine."

"Let me check with the manager. I'm not sure we can fit you in. You see how many people are here."

Bryan's scowl intensified as he watched the hostess walk away. She returned with the manager, who reluctantly told us the best they could do was to sit us at a small round table they would have to squeeze in against the back wall near the kitchen.

"Just do it," Bryan grumbled.

The location of our table was undesirable, but at least we had one. I tried to make light of it. After all, this would be the best evening of my life. What difference did the size and location of the table matter? I waited patiently for Bryan to ask me to dance, but he seemed too disturbed about the lost reservations to enjoy himself. Finally, I asked him to dance.

We made our way over to the dance floor. I was glad to escape from the noisy kitchen area that made conversation difficult and romance almost impossible. The band was playing a slow dance. Now, perhaps, Bryan would relax and remember what this night was all about—two people in love whose lives were about to change forever. We had barely made a few rounds when Bryan suddenly stopped and let go of me.

"Let's go," he said.

"But we just got here," I said as he escorted me off the dance floor. The hostess shook her head as we walked past her on our way out.

At first, I thought Bryan was eager to leave so he could propose to me. Why else would we go so soon? But the weight of his mood dashed all my hopes. By the time we got to my apartment, I was in tears. Everything about this evening had been jinxed—the flowers, the lost reservations, and our unfinished dance. He certainly wasn't going to propose among all these thorns. Maybe he never intended to in the first place. Had I dreamed all this up? I felt like an absolute fool.

Once inside my apartment, I quickly ran to the bedroom and slammed the door behind me. Bryan knocked softly on the door when I didn't return after a few minutes.

"Lori, are you okay?" He said through the door.

"No," I answered.

"Would you come out, please?" Bryan's voice was tender.

I reluctantly opened the door. Bryan took my hand and led me to the sofa. After we sat down, he held me tight against him while I soaked his shoulder with my tears.

"Honey," Bryan said. "Please listen. I love you. Don't be upset. I just wanted everything to be perfect this evening. The only thing that matters is how I feel about you. I mean that."

Bryan brushed the hair out of my eyes, then tilted my head and kissed me. I pulled away from him slightly so we could face each other. He took both my hands in his.

"Lori, will you marry me?" he asked.

I didn't know what to say. Bryan shifted uneasily as the silence between us grew even louder. I had waited all my life for this moment. Now that it was here, all I could think about was the other Bryan.

The Story Behind the Story

"Among the Thorns" was inspired by an incident involving roses delivered to me on the wrong day when my husband and I became engaged. We now laugh when we reflect on all the frustration created by the florist's attempt to redeliver week-old roses. The other details of the story are all fiction, and even the ending, which shows how unpredictable relationships can be and why our choices matter, surprised me. This story was awarded first place in the 2019 Texas Authors Short Stories Contest.

Life is More Than Life

Most would agree that life is merely the time between birth and death. But it's also about being alive, not just physically, but also emotionally and spiritually. Life is energy above all else, which gives credence to the concept of life after life. The only problem is that none of us among the living can speak authoritatively on this subject. Who, in other words, on the planet has any personal experience in this matter? Physicists and theologians agree that when we die, the energy that was us is redistributed as another form—what many perceive as the spiritual nature of the human soul—that continues to live in the infinite.

I am neither a physicist nor a theologian. But I am a writer, and I truly believe that writers play a considerable part in ensuring that the lives of the characters they create continue to live in the hearts and minds of readers forever. In the American classic *A Tree Grows in Brooklyn*, the daily events of a hum-drum life lived below the poverty line were transformed into five hundred pages of brilliant literature. Storytelling is the oldest form of education. Best of all, it teaches life as we live, see, and want it to be. It's possible, I believe, for exceptional art in its many forms to live forever—to continue bringing pleasure, perspective, and pertinence for generations to come.

During the last days that my mother was still alive, she revealed far more about her early life than I had ever known. My mother grew up in the Great Depression, reaching the end of her teen years during World War II. Her family was hardworking but poor. Not once, though, did she ever speak despairingly about a life that I would have found unbearable. During the last weeks of her life, she sang gospel hymns like the ones she had heard growing up. I think those hymns helped her transition from this world to the next. Hearing her sing those same hymns reassured me that life is more than life. My mother's frail, unrefined voice will live in my heart forever.

Aunt Lizzie's Table

"When will we be there?" Keri asked, pressing her face against the backseat window.

"Soon," Mother replied.

There wasn't much to see except cows or goats grazing in pastures. Mostly, there were long stretches of road with pine and cedar forests on either side. Keri and her brother Nate tried to guess what lay hidden behind them.

"Do you think Aunt Lizzie will remember I'm nine years old now?" Keri asked.

"Well, of course, she will," Mother assured her. "Don't worry, Keri. It's your turn to set the table. It's a family tradition for every niece and nephew to help Aunt Lizzie after their ninth birthday."

"It's too bad she never had children of her own," Father added. Aunt Lizzie had four sisters and five brothers. All except her had children, so she had plenty of nieces and nephews to make up for it.

The car pulled in front of the house, and Aunt Lizzie rushed out to welcome them. She spread her arms wide open as Keri and Nate ran toward her.

"It's about time you got here," Aunt Lizzie greeted. "My goodness, Nate, you've grown another foot."

"No, I haven't," Nate answered, looking down to see if he had grown a third foot.

Everyone laughed at Nate's gullibility.

A fluffy white dog with a tail curled over his back darted out of the screen door that opened onto the porch. He was barking loudly and jumping all over Keri and Nate, trying to get them to join him in a romp around the yard.

"Get back in here!" Aunt Penny, one of Aunt Lizzie's sisters, ran after the dog.

"Where did he come from?" Keri asked.

"He belongs to your cousins," Aunt Penny said, "but I'm the one who gets stuck taking care of him."

"He's so cute," Keri said. "What's his name?"

"Star," Aunt Penny said. "Here, you play with him while I say hello to your parents.

"Not now, Keri," Aunt Lizzie said. "Come inside and wash your hands. You can play with Star later on. You know it's your turn to set the table."

Keri followed her aunt inside, past the living room, where her uncle was napping in an oversized chair. From the open windows in the dining room, she could hear Nate and her cousins laughing as they played with Star in the backyard. She wished she could join them instead of helping her aunt.

"Keri, I've set one place so you can use it as an example," Aunt Lizzie explained. "The silver is in the wooden box over there. Just be careful with my fine china. I got every piece of it when I married, and to this day, none is chipped or cracked."

Keri ran her fingers across the white tablecloth to feel the rose pattern woven into the fabric. It was pretty and didn't have a wrinkle in it. She wondered how Aunt Lizzie had managed to iron it. Next, she lifted the lid of the wooden box with all the silverware Aunt Lizzie had polished the day before. Keri wondered if her aunt remembered scolding her a couple of years ago when she and her cousin Lauren decided they needed silver spoons for their tea party.

Keri closed the wooden box and opened one of the corner cabinets. She was about to pick up a stack of plates trimmed with pink flowers and green leaves when Aunt Lizzie stopped her.

"No, dear. I'll bring the plates to the table. You can place them in front of each chair. Please make sure they're nice and straight. The plate determines where everything else will go."

After Keri had neatly placed all the plates on the table, she returned to the wooden box that held the knives, forks, and spoons. The handles on the silverware had pretty edges that ended in little curlicues at the bottom. Keri carefully studied the sample place that Aunt Lizzie had set for her.

"Why do we need two forks?" Keri asked.

"The smaller one on the outside is for the salad. The one next to the plate is for dinner. You always start with the outside fork or spoon and work your way inside. I don't know who figured this out—but it's tradition."

"Do we have to do everything just because it's tradition?" Keri asked.

"You can't make up your own rules without confusing people. That's why we have traditions," Aunt Lizzie replied. "Now, pay attention to what you're doing. Always turn the sharp edge of the knife toward the plate."

Keri finished placing the silverware on the table and noticed that Aunt Lizzie's sample setting had two small plates, one just above the forks and one to the right of the knife and spoon.

"What are these for?" Keri asked.

"The one above the forks is for the salad, and the other is a bread plate. Make sure you do everything exactly as I've shown you. The water glasses go right above the tip of the knife blade. Lastly, you can place the napkins in the center of each plate."

When Keri had finished, she stood back to see what a beautiful table she had set. As Aunt Lizzie placed a flower arrangement in the center of the table, Keri counted fourteen place settings. She called out the names of each person there that day to ensure everyone had a place to sit. There was Aunt Lizzie, Uncle Hank, Mother and Father, Nate, and herself. There was Aunt Penny and Uncle Dale, her cousins Mike and Lauren, and finally, Uncle Walt and Aunt Sara, and her cousins Joey and Claire.

"This table would please a princess!" Aunt Lizzie gave Keri a big hug. She then told Keri she could go outside and play.

Keri looked back as she left, only to catch Aunt Lizzie lining up the forks just a little closer together. Keri didn't mind. Everyone knew that Aunt Lizzie liked everything to be perfect. Besides, all this traditional stuff seemed a bit silly to her.

When it was time to come to the table, Keri ran ahead of everyone. To her surprise, all but one of the napkins she had placed so carefully in the center of each plate was missing.

"What happened?" Keri cried. She looked all around to see if they had fallen onto the floor.

About that time, Star made a mad dash into the dining room, stopping only long enough to stand tall on his hind legs and stretch his neck to grab the last napkin with his teeth. He then ran off with it.

"Come back here, you rascal!" Keri screamed.

Soon, everyone was chasing Star. He circled the table and then under it. No one could catch him. He hurried down the hall, still holding the napkin with his teeth. Everyone followed close behind. He ran into the living room and dropped the napkin on top of the napkins he had snatched earlier. He sat on his hind legs, lifted his head back, puffed out his chest, and howled at the ceiling. Everyone laughed. Star was so proud of himself that no one could be mad at him, not even Aunt Lizzie.

"Look what you've done now. My lovely white linens are ruined." Aunt Lizzie would never think of using paper napkins at her table.

"I know just the thing," cousin Joey declared. He quickly ran down the hallway to a small chest of drawers, which he frequently explored when visiting Aunt Lizzie. He pulled open the top drawer. Inside were several unopened gift boxes of handkerchiefs his uncle had received over the years.

"We can fold these into triangles like the linen napkins," Joey said. He presented them to Keri with a big smile on his face.

Keri and her cousins placed the folded handkerchiefs on the plates. Aunt Lizzie wasn't too happy about it, but no one else seemed to mind. Everyone sat down for dinner. Star came to the table, also, but this time with his head down. He found a spot in the corner where he could take a nap. After all, he was exhausted from being chased.

Keri beamed as Aunt Lizzie thanked her in front of everyone for keeping a family tradition and setting such a lovely table.

When anyone wiped their mouth with a handkerchief, they laughed. And they laughed for years to come when they remembered the story of the disappearing napkins and how a box of gift handkerchiefs had saved the day.

The Story Behind the Story

"Aunt Lizzie's Table" (initially titled "Big Mama's Table") was the first short story I wrote and one of the few that was entirely fictional. It won Third Place for Short Stories, Atlanta Writers Club in 2007. I did not write any other short stories until 2018.

The Universal Language

There is a universal language that everyone knows. No matter where you travel, it is the same. One of my favorite examples of how people from different cultures can connect occurred when I was in Saudi Arabia in the 1980s.

Hofuf is located in the al-Hasa Oasis of Saudi Arabia. It is an ancient city that dates back to Biblical days. It is even rumored that the Queen of Sheba set foot in Hofuf, perhaps on her journey to Jerusalem to meet with King Solomon. The city also has a camel market and plenty of "souqs" where you can find gold, spices, brass pots, baskets, and hand-woven textiles.

As I walked along one of the city streets, an old Bedouin woman selling her wares approached me. She motioned for me to follow her to the curb. I was curious about what she wanted, especially since all the Saudi women in al-Khobar would cross to the other side of the street to avoid me—and never had any of them spoken to me.

The Bedouin woman ordered me to "sit" as she pointed to the curb. It was the only English word she appeared to know, and she repeated it several times until I complied with what she wanted. She placed a "niqab" over my head. It was black with embroidered gold. It was too tight, so I shook my head. As she continued fitting me with various headdresses, a small crowd of Arab men, women, and children gathered around. By then, the old woman had noticed that the eyes peeping out between the veil and "niqab" were blue, like the sky. She gently stroked the skin around the corners of my eyes, expressing her fascination with a lovely sigh. Soon, we returned to haggling over the price of her wares, with the crowd encouraging us to make a deal.

When we finally settled, the Bedouin woman stood up. She took my hand in hers and pulled me up alongside her. "Thank you," she said —the only English words besides "sit" she knew. Everyone applauded. We were all connected at that moment by the big smiles we shared.

Bee Caves Road

It was spring break. Ashley was home from college and couldn't wait to see her best friend, Robin. After having dinner with her parents, who lived about ten miles outside of Austin off of Bee Caves Road, Ashley drove to her friend's apartment. Robin, a junior at the University of Texas, lived north of the campus.

Ashley and Robin spent the evening catching up with one another. When Ashley finally looked at her watch, it was half past midnight.

"Why don't you call your parents and tell them you're staying over?" asked Robin.

"I don't want to do that," Ashley said.

"You shouldn't drive home this late," Robin said.

"My parents wouldn't be too happy if I woke them up in the middle of the night."

"I still think you should stay here tonight."

"I'll be okay," Ashley said as she took her car keys out of her purse.

It was almost one o'clock when Ashley turned onto San Jacinto Boulevard. The usual nighttime traffic had thinned out by the time she passed the UT campus heading South. The sight of the UT Tower always reminded Ashley of the day Charles Whitman fired randomly at anyone on the ground from the tower's observation deck. Her father had watched from the rooftop of his office as terrified people ran and screamed as they tried to escape the gunfire. That was over five years ago, and still, it brought back haunting memories.

As she approached the Texas State Capitol building, the traffic dwindled to almost zero. It seemed eerie to be the only person on the road. Ashley looked in her rearview mirror and saw a vehicle's lights some distance from her. When she stopped at a traffic light, the light-colored pickup caught up with her. Ashley felt safer having someone behind her.

Ashley turned right on 10th Street and continued West toward Lamar Boulevard. The driver stayed close behind her. Now, Ashley was nervous. She told herself that it was coincidental that the driver was taking the same route as she was. When she turned onto Lamar Boulevard, so did the truck. Ashley continued to watch the driver in her rearview mirror. Ashley noted that he was a careful driver, obeying all the traffic rules. He was probably going home after working the late shift. Her imagination was working overtime, she assured herself.

As Ashley drove over the Lamar Boulevard Bridge across the Colorado River, her eyes met the pickup's headlights in the mirror. She turned onto Barton Springs Road, winding her way to Bee Caves Road. The driver stayed close behind. Ashley's heart raced. She had no doubt now that the man was following her.

Bee Caves Road was a four-lane undivided highway that wound its way among the hills west of Austin. Supposedly, its name came from the wild bee colonies that early settlers discovered in nearby caves. There were no businesses, homes, or lighted streets—only emptiness and darkness. Ashley shifted from one lane to another. Whatever she did, the driver mirrored her actions. Ashley pressed down on the accelerator. The man following her speeded up, too, causing her to almost slide off the road on one of the curves.

The driver shortened the distance between her car and his pickup. To maintain control, Ashley reduced her speed in case he rammed her. She then switched to the left lane to prevent him from forcing her onto the shoulder. Or even worse, over a cliff. There was still a long way to go before she reached home. Ashley's parents lived in a relatively new neighborhood off Bee Caves Road. Each house sat on one to three acres or more. The lots were wooded, and the homes were far between one another. Ashley prayed that the man, thinking she could get help once she turned into her neighborhood, would continue down Bee Caves Road.

But when Ashley turned onto the long, winding, two-lane road where her parents lived, the pickup's headlights showed in her rearview mirror. Each house she passed was dark. She couldn't risk trying to get anyone's attention, so she kept driving. The pickup slowed, allowing Ashley to get a few yards ahead.

As Ashley approached her parents' house, she slowed just enough to make the turn onto the gravel driveway. The house was set back several hundred feet from the street. When she was about halfway down the drive, the man in the pickup turned off his headlights and slowly followed her. Her hands sweated as she gripped the steering wheel. She was in extreme danger and had only seconds to figure out what to do.

The garage was on the opposite side of the house from her parents' bedroom. If she blew the horn, they might not hear her. If she got out of her car and tried to run for the door, the man would probably grab her before she could unlock it. And if she stayed put in her car, he might break the windows and drag her out of it.

Ashley looked out over the back lawn, lit only by the floodlights on the corner of the garage. Not far from the backside of the house, the yard sloped several feet. Straight ahead were two pine trees on the top edge of the slope. There was a gap between the trees, but Ashley wasn't sure it was wide enough to drive between them. But what else could she do? She kept going once she reached the end of the driveway, barreling through the pine trees without hitting either one. Once all four tires were on level ground, Ashley veered to the left toward the other side of the house. She gunned the Chevy's engine, drove up the slope, and stopped with the front of her car against the small window of her parents' bathroom. Ashley laid on the horn for dear life.

Ashley's father, startled out of his sleep, came to the window. When he recognized Ashley's car, he raised the window slightly. At the same time, Ashley rolled down her window enough to scream, "Daddy, get your gun!"

"Stay where you are," her father called out to her. He then disappeared. Ashley knew he would have to unlock his gun case and load one of the rifles he mainly used for shooting rattlesnakes.

Ashley's terrified mother came to the sliding glass door so she could watch her while her husband loaded his gun. Ashley feared her mother would unlock the glass door, thinking Ashley could jump out of her car and dash inside. Ashley quickly surveyed the area between the two pine trees and where she had landed her Chevy. The man had not followed her into the backyard. He could be hiding somewhere on foot, waiting for the right moment to assault her.

Ashley realized the dangerous situation her parents were in, too. If the man had a gun, he could shoot all three. More than ever, she wished she had stayed at Robin's apartment. Her father appeared at the sliding glass door. He motioned for her to exit her car as he slid open the door. Ashley rushed inside, bursting into tears as her mother grabbed her. Ashley's mother had called the sheriff while her father watched out the front window. The man had sped off upon seeing a rifle pointed directly at him.

The sheriff arrived and was amazed that Ashley had not crashed into the trees or rolled her car while going down the slope trying to escape.

"You're a very lucky young lady," said the Sheriff. "Can you tell me anything about the driver in the pickup? A description of him, maybe?"

"It was so dark," said Ashley. "I got a glimpse of him at one of the traffic stops. I can only tell you that he was a middle-aged white man. But mostly, all I could see were his headlights following me."

"Was there anything you might have done to encourage him?" asked the Sheriff.

"What are you saying?" asked Ashley's mother. "My daughter could have been raped or killed. Are you accusing her of asking for it?"

"No, ma'am, I'm not. There's been a couple of other incidents like this. I'm just trying to get to the bottom of things. I will say this, though. A young girl shouldn't be driving alone late at night. There're all kinds out there looking for their next victim."

"I've never been so scared," said Ashley.

"Where were you when you noticed he was following you?" asked the Sheriff.

"On San Jacinto just past the Capitol."

"And he followed you all the way out here? He could have forced you off the road. No traffic at this time of night, no place to get help."

"I stayed in the left lane and kept a steady pace. Bee Caves is so curvy. I figured he wouldn't go any faster than I did."

"That was smart of you," said the Sheriff. He then turned to Ashley's father. "Did you get a look at him when you went outside with your rifle?"

"He was too far away," said Ashley's father. "He was already backing out when I came out the door. I'm pretty sure he saw me pointing my rifle at him. He took off like a scared rabbit. All I can tell you is that he was in a GMC pickup, tan-colored, I think."

"I'm going to leave so you all can get some sleep. I'll hang out in the area for a while in case this creep comes back."

"He wouldn't dare, would he?" asked Ashley's mother .

"He knows where you live. But I doubt he'd come back anytime soon. "After the sheriff left, Ashley and her parents sat up for a long time; Ashley, still reeling from her ordeal, her mother worried sick, and her father with the rifle in his lap.

The Story Behind the Story

For me, writing is therapeutic. I based this story on a similar experience as a young girl. The fear of looking in a rearview mirror and thinking someone was following me has stayed with me all these years. But until I wrote this story, I didn't realize how much a split-second decision could determine our fate, whether we are an airline pilot, a surgical doctor, a soldier, a policeman, or a young girl in danger. This story received an award from the Texas Authors Short Stories Awards and Indie Authors Short Story Awards.

Location, Location, Location

When it comes to real estate, location is keen. I think, though, that the same is true regarding writing. By that, I mean the importance of writing what you know—which often involves settings that you are familiar with. That doesn't mean you can't successfully write about environments outside your experience, but it will take more effort.

I am a small-town girl who has lived in large cities in six different states within the U.S. I have traveled to several foreign countries in Europe and worked temporarily in Saudi Arabia. However, I still find that my best writing has some semblance of East Texas in it. Although I had been writing for many years, it wasn't until I moved back to East Texas a few years ago that things fell into place.

First, I wrote a book about Camp Tyler, an iconic Smith County treasure. Next, I finally decided to publish my novel, *The Eyes of the Doe*, which has East Texas all over it. Although Paris (the one in France, not Texas) is the setting of my memoir *Mademoiselle Renoir à Paris*, it's essentially about the adventures of a young East Texas girl. See what I mean?

I recently read that most of an author's writing is drawn somewhat from their experience during the first fifteen years of their life. That's amazing, but I tend to agree. Just recently, a woman contacted me via my website. She wanted advice about how to get started on writing her own story. She referred to herself as a native East Texan. I told her to write what she knows—who and where she is. The biggest mistake some writers make is trying to be somebody other than who they are.

Candy Apple

Marci's coffee turned cold as she slowly combed through the newspaper's special section about the history of the Texas State Fair, which was now underway. She glanced at the black and white photos from years ago till one, in particular, caught her attention.

"Oh, my God," she said. "I can't believe it. Nathan, come here."

"What, another politician doing something scandalous?" Nathan laughed.

"No, you have to see this."

"What's so special about a girl eating a candy apple?" Nathan asked as he peered over his wife's shoulder.

"That's me," Marci replied.

"You? Are you sure about that?"

"Yes, I'm very sure. I remember it well."

Marci had been barely fifteen the first time she went to the state fair in Dallas with her older sister Becky and her brother-in-law Ken. Unlike most of her friends with boys on the brain twenty-four hours a day, Marci spent her time alone writing dark poetry. The year before, she had lost her brother suddenly, leaving her bewildered and tormented. Becky thought it would be good for Marci to do something fun. Marci had reluctantly agreed to go to the fair.

As they entered the fairgrounds, the trio was greeted by Big Tex, who stood over fifty feet high in a roundabout that was cordoned off by a low picket fence. The bow-legged statue wore a red checkered shirt, blue jeans, an oversized silver longhorn belt buckle, cowboy boots, and a large-brimmed Stetson hat. His booming voice could be heard all over Fair Park as he greeted fairgoers and made daily announcements.

Marci didn't care much for the Midway rides. The Scrambler made her dizzy, the Roller Coaster took her breath away, and the Ferris Wheel triggered her fear of heights. The only amusement that she enjoyed was the Carousel. Its lively music was pumped into the air nonstop to attract crowds while drowning out their noise. The only thing louder than the Carousel's band organ was Big Tex.

Becky and Ken were surprised when Marci showed interest in the Swiss Sky Ride, a new addition that carried riders above the fairgrounds in gondola cars that moved across wire cables strung twice as high as the crown of Big Tex's hat. Marci's anxiety about hanging high in the air disappeared once she experienced how grand it was to have a bird's eye view of the fairgrounds.

"Now what?" Becky asked once they were back on the ground.

"I'm ready to see some exhibits," Ken said.

They visited the Freak Show, House of Mirrors, and other side shows featuring magic tricks, daredevil stunts, and fortune-tellers. After they tired of all this, they stopped at several concession stands before going to the exhibit hall, where award-winning cakes and pies, homemade jellies, and other creative arts were displayed.

"I'd like a candy apple," Marci said.

"Didn't you just have a corny dog and some cotton candy?" asked Becky.

"Yeah, but there's nothing like a candy apple."

"Okay, but come right back."

Marci took off toward the concession stands, ignoring the game booth barkers who called out to her. All she had to do was knock over some bottles with a ball. She was sure to win a top prize; they prodded her. When they realized they were wasting their time, they turned their attention to a young boy running ahead of his parents in their direction.

Marci found the booth she had seen earlier with its dazzling display of candy apples with cinnamon, caramel, or peanut-coated shells. She decided on the one with peanuts. It tasted even better than she had expected. Marci began walking back toward the exhibit hall. She focused more on eating her apple than where she was going and lost her sense of direction. As Marci pushed through the crowded Midway, an opening between two concession stands leading to an alley where delivery trucks unloaded supplies caught her attention. A couple of benches were on one side of the alleyway where she could sit while finishing her apple.

A low mass of gray clouds had overtaken the brilliant sun from earlier in the day. The wind had also picked up and blown trash up and down the alley. As Marci bit hard into the apple's candy shell, strands of her windblown hair stuck to it.

In the meantime, Becky and Ken had begun to worry.

"She should have been back by now." Becky looked at her watch again. "What should we do?"

"Why don't you stay here, and I'll look for her," said Ken.

"What if someone kidnapped her?"

"Don't be silly. Marci probably got interested in something and forgot about time."

Ken quickly walked down the Midway until he came to the booth with a large sign that read CANDY APPLES in bold red letters. He went to the counter and spoke to the gruff-looking lady who was busy dipping apples on sticks in warm melted candy.

Excuse me, Ma'am, have you seen a young girl, about fifteen—tall, thin, with blue eyes and long blonde hair?"

"All day long." The gruff lady barely glanced at Ken. "I see lots of young girls that fit that description."

"It would help if you could remember if a young girl like that bought an apple maybe thirty or forty minutes ago."

"Maybe," the lady replied. "I don't have time to look at everyone who comes here. Now, either buy an apple or move on."

Ken walked the entire Midway before returning to the exhibit hall, where Becky waited anxiously for him.

Marci, not realizing how much panic her disappearance was causing, continued eating her apple as if she had all day. Amid the gloom of the clouds and the starkness of the trash-strewn alley, her thoughts took on the same sadness that had inspired many of her poems: the kind that her parents tried to discourage her from writing, the poems that Marci no longer shared with them.

Marci barely noticed the man in the dark gray textured suit with thin, notched lapels who had entered the alley. He was wearing a Fedora hat with a narrow brim and carrying a high-speed press camera with a flashbulb across his shoulder. The man chewed on the remains of a cigar, quietly studying her as she ate her apple, not wishing to disrupt her intense concentration. He began shooting her from different distances and angles when the moment was right. She never blinked or appeared to be self-conscious. It was as though he was hiding behind a curtain rather than being inches from her face.

"Thank you, Miss," the man said before walking away.

For what? Marci wondered. She had almost finished her apple.

Suddenly, she was jolted back to awareness by the unmistakable booming voice of Big Tex.

"Marci Graham, where are you? Your family is looking for you. They're right here at the roundabout with me. Get on over here, Marci!"

Marci got up immediately. She threw what remained of her apple in a trash bin, ran through the opening between the concession stands, and hurried back down the Midway. Big Tex was easy to spot since the only things taller than him were the Ferris Wheel and the Swiss Sky Ride. Becky was almost in tears when she saw Marci coming toward her.

"Where were you?" Becky asked. "We were worried to death."

"I was eating my apple. Didn't know you were looking for me."

"I couldn't find you anywhere," Ken said. "Thank goodness for Big Tex."

The afternoon was almost gone, and it was turning chilly. Becky, Ken, and Marci had had enough of the fair; they all decided. As they were walking out the gate, they heard Big Tex holler, "Ya come back, now."

The Story Behind the Story

Like most stories I write, I took an actual event and turned it into a fictional tale. While eating a candy apple at the Texas State Fair one year, a man photographed me from all angles. I never knew why he took my picture or what he did with the images later. Over the years, I would scan past photos of the fair, hoping that one day I would come across the ones of me and my candy apple. That never happened, so I wrote the story to give my search an ending. "Candy Apple" won an award in the 2020 Texas Authors Short Stories Contest.

My Mother, the Poet

We do not always know someone until they have passed. Such is the case with my mother. I had always believed that if I had inherited a propensity for writing, it came from my father. My father was a storyteller. Although he never told his stories on paper, I firmly believe that storytelling is the heart of all writing.

Once, while sorting through my mother's belongings, I discovered something that puzzled me. Tucked away among the things she held most sacred was a little stash of poems. Structurally, they needed work—primarily due to her awkward attempt at rhyming. They were handwritten with crossed-out words as she struggled to express the most profound sentiments of her soul. The poems were about my brother—the son she lost when he was only fourteen. The raw, aching emotions of my mother's heart jumped out at me. In her words, I saw how determined she was to overcome her grief and how she relied on her faith to accomplish that.

My mother never talked about my brother. She never shared with me or anyone how tormented she was, even though we all knew it. But the words she left behind shouted above all the years of silence. She finally spoke to me on a few pages of crumpled paper.

Cartoon Classics

Raymond Rawlings had a plan. But first, he would have to reinvent himself. He had never done anything like this before and didn't know where to begin. For most of his career, Raymond sold farm equipment. Now that he was retiring, he wanted to be a classical concert booking agent.

Raymond enjoyed listening to classical music while driving down the highway to meet with potential customers in his sales district. He had loved classical music since he was a young boy, watching cartoons on Saturday mornings. Even though Raymond had never been to a live concert, he asked himself, *how difficult could it be?* Raymond had watched enough TV performances to know that the best way to attract an audience is to have the right venue and talent.

Raymond had seen an article in the Dallas paper about a man who had trained as a classical pianist and achieved considerable recognition while still young. Tragically, the man seriously injured himself from falling off a ladder. He could not continue his music career due to injuries to both his arms and hands. But after many years of healing, the man was ready to make a comeback. Already, he was teaching piano in his community.

What a great story, Raymond thought. *If I can get him signed up, he will win the sympathy vote from the audience. Both of us will benefit from his tragedy. And Dallas isn't that far from Waco. I won't have to pay a lot of travel expenses.*

Within two weeks, Raymond had booked Drake Evans, the pianist, as his first musician. Raymond was also busy discussing his plans to implement a series of concerts in the Waco community. He made a pitch to the Waco Chamber of Commerce and other community leaders. There were plenty of online lists of musicians seeking concert bookings. Without much effort, Raymond spotted a Los Angeles flutist and a New York City guitarist. If he could book them, Raymond was sure his venture would succeed. Next, Raymond had to find a venue. That task proved more daunting than booking clients.

Raymond finally stumbled upon an event center used mainly for wedding receptions and art exhibits. It could only seat seventy-five guests inside; however, the outdoor garden would accommodate a larger audience.

"I'd like to book a classical music concert," Raymond told the event manager.

"What date do you want to schedule?" asked the manager.

"Oh, well, I haven't gotten that far yet."

"I can't schedule you without a date. It's first-come, first-served. We do a lot of weddings, especially in the spring. Might I suggest that you consider checking with the Starlite Theatre? They can seat more people than our center."

"Thank you. I will do that."

Over the next few weeks, Raymond contacted potential musicians for his *Premier Classical Concert Series*. Raymond penciled in the flutist and guitarist, though both were reluctant to commit without a written contract.

"Don't worry," said Raymond to the guitarist. "We do things a little differently in Texas. A man's word is as good as gold. I'll go ahead and schedule you for early spring. By then, you'll have a contract. I can't book the concert hall until I have musicians. Do you see what I mean?"

"But what about my travel expenses?" asked the concerned guitarist.

"The details will come later. First, I've got to get top-notch musicians like you on board. You know, to attract the audience that will want to subscribe to the series I'm putting together."

"But I don't know the date I'm to play," said the guitarist.

"Neither do I," said Raymond. "I won't know until I see what's available. Don't worry; we can always change your concert slot if it doesn't work for you."

With that, Raymond continued searching online for other talented musicians for his concert series. Once he had seven musicians lined up, he contacted the Starlite Theatre. The venue had only one opening, which was on Halloween. Raymond reluctantly scheduled Drake Evans, even though he wouldn't have much time to promote the concert since it was just a few weeks away. Next, Raymond contacted the Rose Garden Event Center he had initially consulted. Raymond scheduled one show each month, beginning with December. Raymond took whatever dates were available; most were minor holidays like Valentine's Day, St. Patrick's Day, and

Mother's Day. Next, he put the scheduled performances on a free online events calendar. Since he didn't have the funds to pay for advertising, he hoped people would scramble to book their tickets in advance.

A week before the pianist's Halloween concert, Raymond canceled the performance due to a lack of ticket sales. He rescheduled Drake for a later date in the spring. Raymond then began an active campaign to promote the December through May bookings at the Rose Garden Event Center. He posted an article highlighting the musicians and their scheduled concerts on his new website. Raymond was happy. He was making progress, and the future looked bright.

As December approached, all of Raymond's plans were unraveling. There were no ticket sales for the December concert featuring the guitarist. When Raymond canceled the performance, the guitarist lit into him.

"I don't think you know what you're doing," said the guitarist when Raymond notified him. "I've never had this happen before."

"I don't know what to say," replied Raymond. "I thought you'd be a big attraction; you know someone from New York City. I can reschedule you."

"No thanks. I can't waste my time like this. No musician can. How would you like it if there had been sales and I didn't show up?"

"Okay, I get your point. I admit I'm learning as I go. But my plan is going to catch on eventually. Later on, you might regret not being part of my concert series."

"Don't count on it." The guitarist hung up the phone.

Things continued to go downhill. Tickets were not selling, and the only recourse was to cancel the performances in advance to avoid paying for the event center and other expenses. Without a contract, the musicians were out of luck, too. Still, Raymond believed that things would turn around. He just needed a bit more time to make them work. Raymond began searching for musicians to replace those no longer represented due to cancelations in the Premier Classical Concert Series. He decided to dream big and go after international performers. That should draw a crowd, he concluded.

Raymond also came up with the idea of using the canceled performances to evoke public curiosity. He posted notice of Drake Evans's concert with a slash across it and bold red letters announcing its cancelation due to circumstances beyond his control. Raymond could almost hear people asking: *What happened? It sounded like a good concert. I hope they reschedule him.*

While searching for replacements, Raymond came across a lovely young Japanese woman who played the harp. He contacted Yoshi and found out she lived in Paris. She also mentioned a friend who was a phenomenal French violinist. Raymond started thinking. Travel expenses for bringing international artists to Waco would be expensive. But since the two of them would share the stage, Raymond figured he could reduce their salaries. The violinist, Pascal, contacted Raymond regarding the email he received outlining the concert proposal.

"Monsieur Rawlings, Yoshi, and I have concerns, especially since you are now offering the two of us the same pay you proposed initially to Yoshi as a soloist. You also want us to pay for our travel expenses, which you will reimburse us after the concert if it takes place."

"Pascal, I'm sorry if you think I am trying to cheat you and Yoshi. I wanted to allow both of you an opportunity to make your American debut. I can't do that unless I cut corners somewhere. I'm also talking with Japan Airlines and Air France to see if they are interested in paying for your airfare. You know, as a gesture of international cultural exchange."

"Yoshi and I have noticed that you have canceled several concerts and decreased the ticket price. How do you expect to make money after paying the performers and the concert expenses?"

"What I need is a benefactor. I've been talking to Japanese and French companies based in the U.S., local leaders, art associations, and anyone who would listen. Classical music is not a popular genre, especially in Waco. I'm hoping to change all of that with my concert series."

"I understand," said Pascal. "Yoshi and I must apply for a working visa. That takes time and money. You can imagine how upset we would be if our concert got canceled at the last minute. We spend hours practicing and preparing for every engagement we perform."

"I'm doing everything I can to make this work. That's why I'm moving some of the concerts to later dates. That will give me more time to get the ball rolling, you know, to publicize the series and solicit funds from generous art patrons. I have some good ideas I think would appeal to the upper-crust crowd."

"What do you mean, *the upper-crust crowd*?"

"Society people; those with influence. I plan on having you and Yoshi perform in the rose garden. The seating capacity is twice as much as in the performance hall. And I could have a ballet company perform while the two of you are playing your beautiful music. I also thought about serving some fine wine and recently discovered some high-end cheese. You know, simple but elegant."

"It sounds like you just added more expense. I don't see how you can afford to finance the concerts. And, for Yoshi and me, it is too big of a risk to consider this dream of yours."

"That's my job, Pascal, to manage the whole process. I hope you and Yoshi will accept my proposal. It could be the start of something big for both of you. I promise I'm not trying to scam you."

"Oh, I do not think you are a scammer. But you are a dreamer. The only difference between the two, Monsieur Rawlings, is that a scammer deceives others, and a dreamer deceives himself. Either way, things could go badly for all concerned."

Over the next few weeks, Raymond had to admit he was over his head. Ticket sales were nonexistent; no one he had approached would help sponsor his lofty idea. He feared his inability to fulfill his concert series plan had tarnished his reputation in the community. There was nothing to do but cancel everything.

The following Saturday morning, Raymond sat on the sofa with his grandson, watching cartoon classics like he had done as a boy. Raymond laughed, then sighed as Bugs Bunny sat at a grand piano, comically performing some of Raymond's favorite classical pieces.

The Story Behind the Story

It never occurred to me until recently that my first exposure to classical music came from watching cartoons as a child. Since I have always admired people who retire from one career only to reinvent themselves, I wrote a story based on a man who thought he could be successful at something he loved despite not having the necessary skills or knowledge. While some use skills they've acquired over the years to forge a new career, others are delusional and overestimate their abilities. And many, like myself, become writers charged with capturing the vastness of human nature. This story won an award in the 2021 Texas Authors Short Stories Contest.

Compelling Characters

I think that some of the most compelling fictional characters are those created from actual people—people we know very well or who may have crossed our paths only once but were so memorable we never forgot them. I try to tuck the more memorable ones in the corners of my stories. It's an excellent way to avoid writing stock characters.

One that comes to mind is a lady who was well into her nineties when I met her. The lady was an artist and enjoyed showing me her work, which was quite remarkable. She always came out of her house when she saw my husband and I walking our dog Keiko in Richmond, Virginia. She was petite and bent over, and her whole body shook despite being propped up by a cane. "I've lived so long I'm not afraid of anything. Not anything, I tell you. Not even the devil himself," the tiny woman would boast in her shaky voice when Keiko growled at her if she got too close to us. It was fun finding the perfect place for her in my novel, *The Eyes of the Doe*. She will live forever now.

Empty Mailbox

Sandra and Scott were almost settled in their new home. They had spent months living in an apartment while their house was being built. Finally, they could have all their mail forwarded to their current address. The couple, who had filed their income tax return a while back, expected an income tax refund to arrive any day. They were also waiting on their new driver's licenses and a credit card to replace the one about to expire.

A few weeks after their move, Sandra began to worry that their mail was not being forwarded and that there had been no deliveries for four consecutive days. The next day, however, Scott's driver's license and several pieces of junk mail were in their mailbox.

"That's strange," said Sandra as she handed the mail to Scott. "Why didn't I receive my license?"

"Maybe yours will come tomorrow," said Scott.

"I don't know. We applied on the same day and at the same time. Plus, that's not all that's missing."

"Why don't you check on the other items tomorrow? If they have been mailed, then check with the post office."

The following day, Sandra confirmed that the Internal Revenue Service refund check, the credit card, and her driver's license had been mailed and should have been delivered around the same time as her empty mailbox occurred.

"I'll go to the post office tomorrow," Sandra told Scott when he called her during his lunch break. "Maybe they delivered our mail to the wrong box. Hopefully, whoever received it will return it."

After the morning rush, Sandra arrived at the Post Office a little before ten. She was the only customer, but no one was at the counter, so she had to wait several minutes to get anyone to help her.

"What can I do for you?" asked the clerk when she finally appeared.

"I'm missing several pieces of mail that were sent to me. I confirmed that they should have been delivered by now. We recently moved here, and everything was fine until last week when we stopped receiving mail for four days. Can you please check in the back to see if my mail was returned for some reason?"

"Give me a moment," the young clerk replied as she walked toward the back office.

Sandra grew impatient. It seemed to take a long time for the clerk to find her mail or determine it wasn't there.

"I'm sorry," said the clerk when she returned empty-handed. "I couldn't find anything."

"Well, the mail was not delivered to my address, or someone stole it from my box. Either way, I'd like to file a claim."

"I'll have to get the supervisor," said the clerk.

Sandra waited ten minutes for the supervisor to appear, which only frustrated her more.

"I'm Mrs. Franklin," the supervisor said. "I understand you didn't receive some of your mail. Do you have any documentation that would support your claim?"

"I've contacted the IRS, the DMV, and the credit card company. According to them, the missing items were sent to me."

"Do you have some identification with your current address?"

"We just moved here recently. All I have is the change of address letter from the Postal Service." Sandra pulled the letter out of her purse.

"I'll be right back." Mrs. Franklin disappeared to the back office.

Sandra couldn't help but think her time was being wasted. She tapped her foot impatiently. A short time later, Mrs. Franklin returned holding a stack of envelopes.

"You found my mail?" Sandra breathed easier.

"Is this what you're looking for?" asked the supervisor as she held up the IRS tax refund, Sandra's driver's license, and another envelope from the credit card company.

"Thank you so much." As Sandra extended her hand to receive the mail, Mrs. Franklin stepped back.

"I need to see your driver's license first."

Sandra dug into her purse and pulled out her license.

"No, I'm sorry, this is your former license. I need to see your current one."

"Well, you're holding it in your hand along with my other mail." Sandra couldn't believe what was happening.

"I can't give it to you. Do you have any other identification?"

"Like what? I don't understand why you can't give me my mail. The Change of Address letter shows that my mail was forwarded to our new location."

"All I can do is to mail everything to you. I will inform the carrier to deliver it to you today."

"Why was my mail not delivered for four days? And why did the clerk not find it initially? Something doesn't seem right."

"I don't know. Your mail will be delivered to your box today. You can count on it."

Sandra reluctantly thanked the supervisor and drove home. She kept watch throughout the day for the mail carrier. A little after five, the mail truck turned onto her street. She went outside and stood by her mailbox. Her next-door neighbor was waiting for his mail and walked over to say hello. Sandra shared her story with him as the carrier approached. To her astonishment, the mail carrier breezed past her, stopping at her neighbor's box. Sandra and her neighbor ran over to him as he stuffed several envelopes inside.

"Where is my mail?" asked Sandra. The carrier looked at her as though he didn't know what she was talking about.

"Do you mean your tax refund, credit card, and driver's license?" asked the carrier. "I put it in your box."

"No, you didn't. You just now drove right past me."

"I made a special stop to deliver your mail this morning."

"Why would you go out of your way for one customer?

"I knew how important it was that you got it."

Sandra walked back to her mailbox and opened it. It was empty.

"There's nothing in my box."

"Someone must have stolen it. Sorry, but I've got to finish my route." The carrier sped off before Sandra could say anything.

"I'm going to call the police," Sandra said to her neighbor.

A policeman arrived a half hour later. Sandra told him what had happened.

"Unfortunately, I can't help you," said the officer. "You will have to call the Postal Inspector."

"But he stole my mail," Sandra complained.

"Well, you don't know that for sure."

The next day, Sandra filed a claim with the Postal Inspector. She had her driver's license canceled and a new one to be sent by special delivery.

Her credit card was also canceled, and at least it didn't appear that any charges had been made. The only thing left was to contact the U.S. Treasury Department.

"I'd like to report a stolen tax return," Sandra said to the representative on the phone.

"Was it stolen or lost?"

"In my opinion, it was stolen."

"Opinions don't count. I'm assuming you mean that you never received your refund. Sometimes, it takes longer than we'd like."

"Well, in this case, the Post Office had my return in their possession yesterday but refused to give it to me because I didn't have my new driver's license, which they also had. I would like you to put a stop payment on my tax refund check and issue me a new one."

"I can't do that. We have to wait until the check is cashed before it can be reissued."

"That's crazy," said Sandra. "If someone cashes the check, won't that cost the Treasury Department double? As a taxpayer, I think that's wasteful."

"We will send you some forms to fill out. You and your husband will have to provide your signature twenty times each so we can determine its validity."

"Twenty times? It sounds like we are being investigated while the thief runs free."

"Once the check is cashed, we can send you a replacement. "

It was three months later before the refund check was cashed. The Treasury Department sent a copy of it to Sandra and Scott. The one thing that stood out is that whoever had signed for Sandra had used her maiden name as part of the signature. Sandra noted that her maiden name was only on her driver's license. Anyone cashing the check should have been suspicious of that.

Long after the new tax refund check, driver's license, and credit card were taken care of, Sandra received a summons from a sheriff in a neighboring county. She was to appear in court as a witness in a case involving a woman arrested after being stopped for reckless driving. The woman's car was full of envelopes containing numerous driver's licenses, credit cards, and uncancelled checks. Among them was Sandra's license. The sheriff also included a photo of the woman, who did not look anything like Sandra, to determine if any of the victims knew her. Sandra never went to court, however. The woman made a plea bargain to reduce her jail time.

Sandra and Scott were convinced the woman didn't act alone, but there wasn't enough evidence to determine that. Despite their aggravation, they were just happy that their actions prevented them from any financial loss. And from then on, they would always be wary of an empty mailbox.

The Story Behind the Story

This story is based on actual events and reveals how easily common sense can be thrown out the window. It is also a reminder to pay attention to anything suspicious and take action quickly to minimize loss.

Peace, Prayer, and Poetry

Lately, I have given a lot of thought as to what peace is. We all know the standard definitions: absence of war, harmony with others, tranquility, etc. But none of these describes the peace I have come to know when I write, mainly when I write a poem. All I know is that nothing else really matters. My only need is to express in the best way possible what inspired me to write in the first place. Having found this deep sense of peace, I have discovered that I no longer have to wait for peace to write; peace comes from writing itself. And once you're in that zone, the writing becomes as easy as breathing.

The Hebrew word for peace is shalom. The root of this word means "that which is complete or whole." It is a better description of my feelings than those mentioned above. When writing, I feel complete: not lonely, not afraid, not worried, not disturbed, not lacking in any way.

Like a prayer, a poem can be a reflection, a meditation, or a thanksgiving. Some poems express beauty or creation, while others seek to unite us in our human experience or understand our world. When I write, I often feel I have access to the Divine, best described as inspiration (or the breath of God). We all have it but don't always realize or act on it.

Some say that people write poems because they can't help it. To a degree, I think that's true. But without peace, it's a struggle. With peace, it's total bliss.

Escape From Iran

Laura and Megan became good friends in the late 1970s while sharing a carpool organized by Laura's father and two co-workers to help reduce Houston's long lines at the gas pump, high prices, and local air pollution.

Laura had met her boyfriend, Rashid, during her senior year of college. Rashid, whom everyone called "Rich," had received a scholarship from the Iranian Navy to study in the United States. Upon graduation, he returned to his home country.

Later on, Laura joined Rich in Tehran, where they married. Not long after, Laura and Rich were expecting their first child. Laura decided it would be better for her to return home for the delivery. She would stay in her parents' home in Houston, which was no longer occupied. Laura's mother had passed away a couple of years ago, and her father had remarried after Laura relocated to Iran. He and his new wife lived in her home.

Megan was glad to have her friend back in Houston and frequently stayed overnight at Laura's home, especially as Laura's due date drew near. Laura was upset about her father's hasty marriage to his secretary, and being so far away from Rich didn't make matters any better.

"Guess what? Rich is coming to Houston soon," announced Laura when Megan stopped by one day.

"That's fantastic," said Megan.

"Well, I think the baby will be here before he arrives."

"Still, that's better than not at all."

"I'm surprised the Navy is giving him a leave of absence."

"Why is that?"

"There are rumblings. Some think the country is going in the wrong direction; too Western for many tastes. I'll feel better once he's here. I hope nothing happens before he gets away." Laura sighed, placing her hands on her swollen belly.

In the meantime, Megan was having problems with her lungs collapsing spontaneously. She had already had surgery to help prevent any future collapses on one of her lungs. The day before Laura's baby girl was born, Megan was on bed rest while recuperating from another collapse. Managing without Megan made life more difficult for Laura. She counted the days before Rich would be in Houston for three months. But once he was in the States, she was sure he would want her to return to Tehran once his leave ended.

There was much celebration when Rich came home to his wife and daughter, Kayla. Not only were they together as a family, but several Iranians Rich knew visited them regularly. Most were seeking advanced degrees or working for the various oil companies in Houston. Megan enjoyed being with Rich's friends and especially liked it when Laura played her guitar while singing "Guantanamera." Even though the lyrics were in Spanish rather than English or Farsi, its haunting melody seemed understood by all present as a song about sharing verses or poems of the soul. Everyone felt connected when they joined Laura in singing the refrain.

Still, much of their talk was focused on what was happening in Iran. Just two weeks after Rich arrived in Houston, the Shah of Iran fled the country as his regime fell apart. Within a month, the 1979 Islamic Revolution began. The Shah's arch-foe, Ayatollah Khomeini, took over, and everything changed dramatically.

Many Western expats exited the country as fast as possible, and numerous Nationals followed suit. Some left on foot through the mountains, hoping they would survive the journey. Rich wondered what he should do; having his wife and daughter return to Iran with him was out of the question. He needed an extension of his stay until things settled down.

"Let me ask you something," said Rich one day when Megan visited him and Laura. "What happens when your lung collapses?"

"In my case, small sacs ruptured and leaked air into the space between my chest wall and lung." Megan was curious as to why Rich was interested in her health.

"Were there any symptoms?"

"Shortness of breath and chest pain."

"But no one could look at you and know that you had a collapsed lung, could they?"

"I suppose not. Why are you asking?"

"I need your help. If I don't return to Iran after my leave is up, I would be considered a deserter, which is punishable by execution. But maybe, if I had a medical reason that prevented me from flying, I could stay here long enough to figure something out."

"But you don't have a medical condition," said Megan, confused.

"Could your doctor write a letter stating that I couldn't fly due to a collapsed lung?"

"No, he would never do that. Besides, that's illegal."

"Then my only choice is to never return to Iran. I may never see my parents or siblings again."

"Well, maybe I could write a letter for you."

"But you aren't a doctor."

"What I mean is that I would write a letter that appears to be written by a doctor."

"Isn't that illegal, too?"

"It depends on how you look at it. The letter is not intended for anyone in the U.S. I don't think anyone would care if it was sent to Iran."

"But how would you do it?"

"Leave that to me," said Megan.

That evening, Megan took the supplies she needed to create a letterhead from her desk drawer. But first, she needed to come up with a made-up physician's name and address, then decide what she would say in the letter. Once that was determined, she peeled off adhesive letters of the alphabet from a vinyl page, transferring them to the sheet of paper with the letterhead. It took a few attempts to get everything looking perfect. Megan handwrote the body of the letter addressed to the fake doctor, hoping that she was familiar enough with the medical terminology from her experience with collapsed lungs to convince whoever received the letter in Iran. Megan was pleased with her creation and hoped Rich would be, too.

"It looks professional," said Rich when Megan showed the letter to him the next day.

"Who will you send it to?" asked Megan.

"I'll have to think about that, but one of the admirals for certain."

"Of course, if they check out the name and address of the physician, you will be in serious trouble."

"I have no choice but to give it a try. I won't leave my wife and daughter, nor can they return to Iran with me. Besides, I've only a few days of leave left."

"So, if you don't go back to Iran, they will consider you a deserter. You could always seek asylum. You and your family would be protected."

"Yes, but what would I do? How would I make a living?"

"I don't know, but I think you would do well no matter what."

Several weeks passed after Rich mailed the letter. He never heard anything back, so he was sure he was now considered a traitor. If he ever set foot in his home country, his life would be ended quickly. What he hated the most was that he couldn't contact any of his family members, who must have been frantic after not hearing from him. His only hope was that one day, they would learn that he, his wife, and his baby daughter were safe and doing well.

Over the next few months, the Shah traveled to several countries before entering the United States in October for cancer treatment. Islamic militants were enraged and responded by storming the U.S. Embassy on November 4, 1979, which resulted in fifty-two American hostages being held for four-hundred-and-forty days. In March 1980, the Shah received asylum in Cairo, Egypt, where he died on July 27, 1980.

Anti-Western sentiment in Iran led to Islamic codes of dress and behavior that had been almost done away with under the Shah's regime. New laws influenced by Islamic codes were implemented, and religious committees patrolled the streets to ensure everyone complied. The most affected group was women. Numerous rights granted during the Shah's reign were taken away. Women were now required to wear a veil and were deemed submissive to male family members. Alcohol was banned, and so was listening to Western music.

Eventually, Rich, with the help of Iranian friends now living in the United States, opened a carpet/rug gallery. He was familiar with this business since several of his family members back home were Asian rug dealers. Rich was quite successful and even hired Megan to work for him as his bookkeeper.

Over the years, Megan lost track of Laura and Rich, but she thought about them frequently. Any mention of Iran reminded her of her letter, hoping to help Rich avoid the consequences of not returning to his country. Even today, many of those, like Rich, who managed to escape from Iran during the 1979 Revolution, cannot return to their country. I think Rich made the right decision, and most likely, he has enjoyed a wonderful life in the United States.

The Story Behind the Story

Although this story is based on an actual event, all names, dialogue, and incidents have been fictionalized. More than anything, the story reminds us of the freedoms we often take for granted. It is also a story of triumph. Leaving your country and family takes courage and even more courage to start a new life. One day, I hope to reconnect with my former friends. They will always live in my memories, no matter what.

Keiko's Leash

Our first dog, Keiko, taught me many things. This story is one of them. Many years ago, Bob was offered a job in Virginia. We looked forward to the move, but it did mean I would have to stay behind for a while. The real estate market in Houston was down, and it looked like it would take a long time before we had a buyer. I didn't want to stay in Houston alone, so I packed everything and stored it.

One night, about a week before our move, I noticed that our dog Keiko had scratched a small opening in a carpet seam. The hole was in the center of the room where a piece of furniture could not hide it. I tried repairing it by cutting a piece of spare carpet the size of the opening to plug the hole. Not satisfied with my first attempt, I cut a new carpet section and widened the original gap to make it fit. This process continued until I found myself staring at a twelve-inch hole. The following day, I made a frantic call to a carpet company and arranged for someone to come and fix the mess I had made.

When the repairers were gone, I vacuumed up all the scraps they had left behind. I had put Keiko on a leash to keep her out of the way. Before I knew it, I had sucked the end of her leash into the vacuum. Terrified, Keiko began running in the opposite direction while I chased her, screaming hysterically. I struggled to keep up with her in our wild chase around the room to avoid choking her neck. I was so focused on making Keiko stop running that I failed to realize I had complete control over what was happening. All I had to do was to turn off the vacuum. Sometimes, we make things more complicated than they must be by controlling everyone's actions but our own.

Farewell Champayne

I hesitated before walking up the stairs to the second-floor balcony. I wondered if I had made the right decision. I had been coming here for five years, often once a week. Although I had set the end date, I wasn't sure it was what I wanted to do. I remember the first time I met Patrick. I stood up in the waiting room when he called my name. He placed his hands together like a prayer and bowed slightly. At that moment, I was captivated by his mystical and enchanting gesture.

Patrick was my analyst. Other than his age, I knew nothing about him. I could never break through his psyche, no matter how much I tried. Whenever I asked him about his personal life, he would respond by asking me to reveal who I thought he was. What I made up in my stories provided more clues about my inner nature than his. Patrick always upheld boundaries that kept him from stepping into the traps I set. The fact that he was only two years older than me and very handsome made it even more difficult for me to avoid fantasizing about having a romantic relationship with him.

I began therapy after finally realizing that I had never let go of losing my brother when I was fifteen. I had carried this burden everywhere I went and imposed it on every meaningful relationship I was in. Even time had not diminished the ache I felt in my heart. When I returned from a two-week trip visiting friends in The Netherlands and England, away from my current boyfriend and other people who had disappointed me, I decided to deal with my unsatisfactory circumstances.

I never expected to continue with treatment as long as I did. But one thing led to another. The more I engaged in the process, the more I learned about myself. There were times when I broke down from the weight of my sorrow. It was too much, spilling over into other areas of my life. I wasn't sure if I would ever be whole. How could I if I had never been complete in the first place? Patrick became the only stable person I knew. He never judged me, never made me feel that I was too far gone to get over myself.

Even though I was progressing, I still had things wrong. I was looking for the perfect relationship while hanging on to the current one. As miserable as I was, having someone in my life was more satisfying than being alone. And although my relationship with Patrick was not based on reality, it lessened the pain of my inner world. Still, it took three years before I was ready to dissolve my failing, long-term relationship without any strings attached. I was finally free but still unsure of what lay ahead.

It wasn't long before I met someone entirely different from anyone I had ever been involved with. I felt appreciated and confident in myself. Three months later, I was engaged to be married. Although I was happy beyond words, I chose to continue with my therapy sessions. After attending my wedding, Patrick later told me he had felt like he was "giving me away" at the ceremony. So often, I told Patrick I would rather sit on the sofa sharing a glass of champagne than tell him all my issues. Although he never commented on what I said, I never felt rejected.

But here I was, in early December, about to experience my last counseling session. Was I truly ready for this? Patrick opened the door to the sitting room, signaling for me to enter.

I stopped mid-way, startled at what I saw. There was an ice bucket with a bottle of champagne and two glasses beside it. I didn't know what to say.

"Have a seat." Patrick gestured at the sofa.

Everything seemed surreal.

"Would you like a glass?" Patrick continued as he popped the cork of the bottle.

"I can't believe you did this," I said.

"It's a day to celebrate." Patrick filled my glass. He smiled as he handed it to me and gently touched my hand—something he would have never done before.

We talked about all the time we had shared and how much my life had changed. As we sipped the champagne, tears rolled down our cheeks. Although saying goodbye was painful, it was comforting to acknowledge that our relationship was perfect and complete. I felt at peace for the first time in my life.

I was just as hesitant about leaving as I had been about arriving. Patrick stood up and hugged me as I rose from my seat. It was a gesture so longed for; met somewhat with restraint. Letting go of Patrick on my terms and timetable was healing and symbolic of the goodbye I never had when my brother died.

Patrick stood on the balcony as I walked down the stairs for the last time. I looked over my shoulder and waved goodbye, knowing I would never return. I now knew the importance of embracing grief rather than denying it, as I had done for many years.

I thought about Patrick over the next few months but resisted contacting him. Six months later, however, a women's group I belonged to was interested in having a psychologist speak at one of their meetings. I suggested Patrick, and everyone agreed.

I was excited about having a good reason to contact my former therapist. I had missed him, but I knew how important it was for me to let go of our relationship. I was surprised by the unfamiliar voice on the other end of the phone.

"Is Patrick there?" I asked.

"I'm afraid you have the wrong number."

"No, I don't think so." I gave the man who had answered Patrick's last name.

"I don't know anyone by that name."

"He was my former psychologist. He practiced with another man, whose name I can't remember."

"I've been here since May. I took over the practice of another man who moved to California. He's not the man you are looking for, but perhaps he would know Patrick's whereabouts. I will get back to you once I have contacted him."

"I would appreciate that." It concerned me that Patrick and his partner had vanished without my knowing. Why hadn't Patrick informed me?

I did not hear from the man I had spoken to for two weeks. When I answered his call, he seemed hesitant to say anything.

"I'm so sorry to tell you this, but Patrick passed away a few months ago."

"That can't be true. Are you sure you spoke to the therapist he worked with in Houston?" I was stunned.

"I'm very sure. I wish I could give you more details, but I can't."

"Was it an accident, or did someone kill him?"

"No, all I know is that he was in the hospital for over a week before he died."

"I'm devastated."

"Is there anything I can do for you? If you need to talk, you have my number."

"Thank you. I need some time, is all."

I searched for an obituary, but there was none. I began to wonder if Patrick was make-believe. I knew nothing about him; it was as though he had come into my life when I needed him, then vanished once I no longer did. It occurred to me that had this happened when I was undergoing therapy, what an even bigger mess my life would become.

It was many years later before I had some closure. Upon moving to Atlanta, we joined the Unity Church. The current minister was an associate minister formerly at the Unity Church in Houston, where Bob and I had met and were married. While participating in a group led by the minister in Atlanta regarding people who had helped us on our life's journey, I shared my story about Patrick.

"What was Patrick's full name?" asked the minister. He had a strange look on his face.

He was quiet for a few moments after I gave it to him.

"I officiated his memorial service," he spoke softly.

"But he didn't attend Unity. I don't understand."

"Several of Patrick's friends arranged the memorial service. He didn't go to Unity, but his friends felt that it was the place he would have wanted to have it."

I remembered all the times I had spoken about the Unity Church during my sessions. Plus, Patrick attended my wedding there. I suddenly felt that his service was held in that spot because of me, that the things I shared with Patrick impacted him, just as he had with me. It all seemed holy in some way.

My heart ached that I had not been informed about Patrick's death. There must have been an obituary, but I could never find it. How could I have spent five years with someone, sharing every aspect of my life, yet knowing nothing about him but his age? Perhaps that was remarkable: the perfect psychologist who stayed in his lane one hundred percent of the time. Patrick was a paragon among men. I never forgot him, and I never will. It is because of him that I am here now.

The Story Behind the Story

When I began writing this story, the only things I knew about Patrick were his age and that his memorial service was held at the Unity Church in Houston, Texas. I had even forgotten his last name. Then, in the middle of the night, I awoke with his name almost screaming at me. The first thing I did the following day was to go online and search for any information available. To my surprise, an obituary with Patrick's photo popped up after being included in the Texas Obituary Project. Finally, I had his death date, cause of death, and his burial site in Ohio. I found his tombstone engraved with these words: "The wise man discerns neither creation nor destruction, only change." Farewell, dear Patrick, farewell.

My Short-Lived Life as an Artist

I was born an artist. At least, that's what everyone told me. And though I tried my best to live up to other people's expectations, I didn't see myself in that role. Before I had even begun school, I won an art contest (of sorts). A local TV show would read a children's story over the air and then ask viewers to draw a picture to go along with it. The story that week was "The Boy and the North Wind." My picture won. I received a copy of the book as an award.

All through school, my teachers praised my artwork. When I was sixteen, my mother signed me up for art classes at the Dallas Art Institute. I was the only "child" in the class. All the other students were studying art for a living. I usually spent eight hours, two days a week at the Institute. I got to work on a project that involved researching period costumes from around the world for a window display at the Sanger-Harris Department Store in Dallas. I spent hours studying every aspect of a horse's structure and how they move before I could draw one. After my art instructor forwarded my interior designs to a prominent interior decorator in Dallas, I received a letter from him offering me an internship once I finished high school. I never followed up on it.

During my first semester of college, I was an art major. But I soon grew impatient and insecure about my ability to continue down this road. That was the end of my artistic career. Many years later, I taught elementary students art appreciation (as a volunteer). I found that very satisfying, and I probably learned more about art from that experience than any other.

When it came to writing, I took the long road to get there. I didn't bother to learn the craft. I didn't work diligently to write stories and poems. In my mind, I was born a writer. What more did I need to do? I now know the answer to that. And while I regret not recognizing it sooner, there's nothing more satisfying than waking up each day eager to work on whatever it is you love to do. It's never too late to become the person you were born to be.

Final Curtain

Margaret Thistle waited for the sixth chime of the grandfather clock before throwing off her covers and sitting on the edge of her bed. She pressed her toes into the plush-lined slippers she had positioned beside her bed the night before. The wood floor creaked as she walked across the room to her closet. Margaret dressed quickly, choosing something appropriate from her small wardrobe for that day's activities. She then pulled back the gossamer curtain of the large window that faced an oak-shaded street. Light flooded her bedroom, which, over time, had darkened with age. Margaret stared through the glass as though seeing another time filled with people she had loved and lost, places she had been, and a medley of things that had happened along the way. She thought about her late husband and the son they had lost in Vietnam. She thought about her wayward daughter, who barely spoke to her anymore. Margaret went through the same routine every morning. And every morning, she felt lonely and tired of living.

Sometimes, she would wander over to the antique secretary stationed in the little nook next to the closet. She would always hesitate before opening its drop front desk, unsure if she wanted to unearth its secrets. She would take the ornate brass key hidden in a leather pouch in one of the desk's cubby holes and unlock the center door. Inside was a stack of faded envelopes tied together with a blue satin ribbon. Margaret would carefully hold them to her breast before placing them against her lips—their faint mustiness a reminder of how long they had been hidden away. She would then close her eyes and remember the most memorable moment of her life. Something she kept buried deep in her heart, something she still had difficulty believing had ever happened. Something that still felt as splendid as it had over thirty years before.

Even though she had been well over fifty back then, she had looked younger. Still, she had been past the age when men would look her way and find her beautiful or captivating. Yet, even now, just as then, there was a hint of the beauty time had faded in her piercing eyes, her delicate lips, and the highlights in her hair that hid any signs of graying. To her advantage, age had sharpened her senses, had made her more interesting, and, unexpectedly, very attractive. The sadness she suffered from losing her son had long since melded into a tenderness that was often mistaken as affection.

After their son died, Margaret and her husband Harold grew apart. Harold, an attorney, threw himself into his work, spending long hours at his office and then shutting himself in his study each night to pore over client files. Margaret busied herself with the Women's Symphony League and the Blue Bonnet Garden Club.

One summer evening, her life changed out of the blue. The symphony league had booked a chamber orchestra, a quartet with a flute, violin, cello, and viola, for the garden club's annual party. With her vast knowledge of classical music, Margaret had helped plan the event and was influential when selecting the orchestra. Having a quartet on tour from Germany would undoubtedly attract new members for the garden club and the symphony league. Everyone was talking about it.

The evening of the event, Margaret was eager to speak the limited French she knew with two of the orchestra members from Paris, who were frequently asked to tour with the Cologne Chamber Orchestra.

"*Bonsoir*," she greeted them. "*C'est un plaisir de vous rencontrer.*"

"*Merci, Madame.*" The young violinist kept his eyes on Margaret. "We are happy to be here. Thank you for inviting us."

"You speak English extremely well," Margaret observed.

Following the concert, Margaret and several other symphony league members engaged in lively conversation with the musicians. Margaret was glad that Harold had opted not to attend the performance, as he would have insisted that they leave as soon as it ended. Most of Margaret's conversation was with the violinist, who must have been half her age. But he was charming, and they had much in common. Margaret offered to send copies of the photos she had taken that evening if any of the musicians were interested. Jules, the violinist, gave Margaret his address. The delightful evening ended with alternating kisses on the cheek. Margaret couldn't help but notice that Jules had pulled her a little closer to him when they were saying goodbye.

As soon as Margaret's film was developed, she selected several photos and mailed them to Jules, along with a note about how much she had enjoyed meeting him and hearing the quartet's beautiful music. Of course, the haunting sounds of the violin were what she remembered almost as much as his tender embrace.

To her surprise, Jules wrote back, making several inquiries about her life that would require a polite response. Margaret tucked the letter away in the desk drawer, unsure if she should mention it to her husband. It seemed innocent enough, but Harold might not think it was a good idea for her to answer Jules's letter. But she wanted to and would think of a way to ensure his response. Jules and Margaret began corresponding regularly, each letter becoming more intimate. At Margaret's request, Jules used the name Juliette in his return address so Harold would think the letters were from a former pen pal who now lived in Paris. But since Harold paid little attention to what Margaret did, the letters went unnoticed.

Margaret always used her finest linen stationary when writing to Jules. And her best ink pen to showcase her skillful handwriting. Sometimes, she would dot the edge of the page with lavender, hoping its delicate scent would survive the journey to Paris. The letters became the highlight of her life, and she would drop everything to read each one when they arrived. She was stunned when the words from one of his letters jumped out at her: "Come to Paris, my darling." Surely not. But the thought of it lingered in her mind for several months. She contacted her former friend who lived in Paris, informing her that she was planning a trip the following month. Traveling to France to see her friend would be her cover. Harold would certainly be okay with that. And so Margaret began making plans.

In early summer, Margaret flew to Paris. She and Jules spent the entire two weeks together, strolling along the Champs-Élysées, sipping expresso at sidewalk cafés, dining by candlelight, and making love. Margaret had never been more fulfilled. But she could make no sense of what she felt. Here she was, a woman in her fifties, acting like a schoolgirl with a man half her age. What did he see in her? "Age does not matter when you love someone," Jules repeatedly told her. "Why do you concern yourself with such nonsense?" Regardless, Margaret had her doubts. She would never leave Harold. Margaret had a comfortable life and a husband who loved her. What could Jules promise her other than romantic, sensual love that would eventually fade away, in particular after she grew older? "No," she told herself. "This must end."

She returned home and wrote one last letter to Jules. He responded, pleading with her not to let their love end this way. Margaret did not answer him, and she never heard from him again. But she did not forget him either. Not long after, Harold died suddenly of a heart attack. And even though she was now an unmarried woman, free to do as she pleased, she did nothing but instruct her attorney to keep track of Jules's address each year. And then she updated her will.

When Margaret passed away at eighty-seven, her attorney immediately located Jules, who still lived in Paris. Margaret's instructions were exact. She was leaving her entire estate to Jules, other than a small portion for her estranged daughter, under one condition: Jules was to play his violin at her funeral.

And so Jules arrived in the United States a few days later with his violin and a heavy heart. He had never forgotten his time with Margaret many years before. He was now a little older than Margaret's age when they had met. The piece Margaret had specified she wanted him to play was the Chopin *Variation, Prelude in B Minor*, a work played at Chopin's funeral. Although written for piano, Margaret preferred an arrangement accompanied by a violin. And that was what she wanted Jules to play.

There was only a small gathering for Margaret's service. Her attorney handed Jules a note when he arrived. Jules recognized the beautiful handwriting on the envelope. He carefully opened it and pulled out the familiar stationery that Margaret always used when writing him. His heart was filled with longing as he read her words.

> My darling violinist,
> One day, many years from now,
>> Perhaps you will look up into the sky
>> And you will see a bright, shining star,
> And you will know that it's me
>> Looking down and watching over you.
> All my love, M.

He placed the note in his vest pocket, close to his heart. And when it was time for the Chopin piece to begin, Jules looked out at the small audience as his eyes filled with tears. The pianist commenced Chopin's haunting melody as Jules lifted his violin and placed his cheek against its rest. Jules closed his eyes as his bow touched the strings, evoking the most beautiful music he had ever played. In his heart, he knew Margaret was smiling down at him.

The Story Behind the Story

The inspiration for "Final Curtain" was a portrait painted by my cousin, Cynthia Ross Vermie. The painting depicted an older woman looking out a window as she clutched the gossamer curtains she had pulled aside. Her eyes were filled with sadness, as though she was peering into her past. At the same time, I was listening to one of my favorite pieces, a Chopin Variation featuring a violin like the one in the story. And finally, I had recently returned from Paris, retracing my journey there as a young girl. The story evolved from these combined elements and was awarded First Place in the 2018 Texas Authors Short Stories Contest.

Dreams, Decisions, and Destinations

When writing *The Sand Rose*, a novel based on my experiences in Saudi Arabia, I came across a stack of letters I either wrote or received during my stay many years ago. The notes provided helpful insight, but more than anything, they made me realize how many different directions my life could have gone. The things we ignore, the things we explore, and the things we adore all play a significant role in our life's direction.

One of the letters contained a quote from American poet Edwin Arlington Robinson, who won the Pulitzer Prize for his work Tristram in 1928. When I read the passage, it struck me as one of the most beautiful verses I have ever read. I don't remember the person who sent it to me, but we must have shared a meaningful relationship on some level. Many times, we ignore what is right in front of us. Or we tend to explore other options to see what else is out there. But at some point, who or what we adore determines our destiny.

The title of the poem is "The Star-Treader," and the lines included in the letter I received long ago are shared below:

Leave me to the stars . . . they must be more than fire,
And if the stars are more than fire
What else is there for them to be but love?

I have no regrets about how my life turned out, for "if the stars are more than dead, what else is there for them to be but light?"

Flashover in Vegas

Sully Filmore was a wealthy cotton farmer from Yazoo City, Mississippi. He and his wife, Frankie, traveled frequently and were regular passengers aboard the Delta and Mississippi Queens, which crossed up and down the Mississippi River between the Port of New Orleans and St. Paul, Minnesota.

But this year, they would celebrate their fiftieth wedding anniversary and wanted to go somewhere they had never been. Sully and Frankie finally decided on Las Vegas, Nevada, and booked a room at the MGM Grand Hotel, which had opened in 1973 as one of the world's largest and most luxurious state-of-the-art hotels.

The couple flew out on November 20, 1980. Their anniversary wasn't until the twenty-second, but they wanted plenty of time before and after to enjoy the entertainment offered on the Las Vegas Strip.

Sully always stood out in a crowd, especially when he wore his navy-blue blazer topped off by a neat, red bowtie. His thinning hair was combed back, Anthony Hopkins style. And even though he appeared somewhat dignified, one couldn't help but sense a bit of the devil in him.

After checking into the MGM Grand on their first evening, Sully and Frankie had dinner at one of its upscale restaurants. Tired from their long flight, they went to bed early.

Around seven a.m., there was a frantic knock on their door. Frankie was still getting dressed, and Sully was busy adjusting his hearing aids while trying to figure out the loud noise that sounded like helicopters hovering over the hotel.

Sully opened the door, startled to see a barefoot woman with wet hair and only a towel wrapped around her middle.

"There's a fire," the woman screamed.

"I didn't hear any alarms," Sully replied.

"There weren't any!" The woman's voice grew even more high-pitched. "I ran out of my room without my key and got locked out."

"Get inside." Sully could now smell the smoke that had spread via the return air plenum, stairwells, elevator shafts, the HVAC units, and the seismic joints of the building.

Sully opened the closet, pulled out his new, expensive suede leather coat, and handed it to the woman as Frankie came out of the bedroom to see what was happening.

"There's a fire," Sully said. "Probably just a kitchen blaze; otherwise, they would have sounded the alarms."

"I don't think so," the woman said. "I saw a big cloud of smoke rising past my window. We're on the tenth floor, and that's pretty high up."

The twenty-six-story luxury hotel had three wings built over a casino, restaurants, showrooms, and a convention center. Many guests in the hotel's 2,076 guestrooms were still sleeping or unaware that a fire had been raging below inside the building's belly for nearly an hour.

"We're going to die, aren't we?" Frankie looked over at Sully.

"Don't talk like that." Sully scolded. "Tomorrow's our anniversary, and we've made it this far. I promise you; we're not going to die."

"Oh my God," the woman said, pointing to the smoke seeping under the door.

"Fill up the tub," Sully said, "and soak some towels."

As Sully began closing the heavy draperies to help seal the windows, he saw glass raining from above. Although the emergency responders had already contained the fire, the hotel towers were like chimneys, drawing smoke and toxic fumes into the upper floors. Many of the guests, Sully assumed, were breaking out windows to escape the heat and smoke in their panic, not realizing that they could be tragically met by the smoke outside the hotel that was being sucked in through the broken windows.

After placing the towels around the bottom of the door, Sully, Frankie, and the woman sat quietly, waiting for someone to rescue them, but no one came. And apparently, no one had activated the hotel's manual alarm system, allowing the smoke to continue racing up the towers unannounced. Also, the building complex was only partially sprinkled, mainly in the convention areas, showrooms, and some of the restaurants on the Casino level, the Arcade levels, and part of the twenty-sixth floor.

"Can the fire truck ladders reach us?" Frankie asked.

"I don't know," Sully said. He walked to the plaque by the door and read the emergency instructions. Although there were six stairways in the high-rise tower, guests were cautioned that they could not access other floors once they entered the stair enclosures.

"What are we going to do?" asked the woman.

"Well, ladies, I'm concerned about what we might find in the stairways. But we can't sit here, either."

"There're balconies on the other side of the building," the woman said. "My room had one."

"Yeah, but you're locked out," Frankie said. "Even if we got to a balcony, we'd need a helicopter to pluck us off."

"We don't have much choice," Sully said. "We can die in this room or die trying to escape. I vote for the latter."

The trio covered their faces with wet towels and entered the smoke-filled corridor. At the same time, firefighters climbed over dead bodies as they made their way up the stairwell to the tenth floor. Just as Sully passed out and lost consciousness, a fireman rushed into the hallway and slapped an oxygen mask across his nose and mouth. Other rescue workers placed oxygen masks on Frankie and the woman, then escorted them down the smoke-filled stairway until they reached one of the lower floors, where a firetruck ladder could safely evacuate them. If it hadn't been for her dazed condition, Frankie would have insisted on staying with her husband, following him even to her death.

Two firefighters used an ax to open the door of a room across the hall with a balcony. They carried Sully outside and signaled one of the helicopter pilots circling the hotel to lower a gurney. After securing Sully to the stretcher, the firefighters motioned for the pilot to lift him from the balcony. Within minutes, Sully arrived at the emergency room and was immediately treated for smoke inhalation. Once on the ground, Frankie and the woman were taken by ambulance to the hospital, where Frankie and Sully were kept overnight for observation. The woman, whose name Sully and Frankie never knew, was released later that evening. They never saw her again, nor did she return the suede leather coat Sully had loaned her.

The following day, the *LA Times* featured Sully, identified as the first victim transported from one of the tenth-floor balconies, dangling from a helicopter lifeline. After being released from the hospital, Sully and Frankie returned to the MGM Grand to examine the damage.

"What balcony were you on?" a reporter asked who had overheard Sully talking about his helicopter rescue.

"Go find the balcony with the biggest puddle on it, and that's where I was!"

From that day forward, Sully carried the newspaper clipping of his rescue in his back pocket. Whenever he checked into a hotel, he would pull it out and slap it on the counter if the desk clerk tried to put him above the sixth floor.

"Not on your life!" he would inform them.

Over the next few days, details about the fire began to surface. Most victims were found above the twentieth floor, about as far from the actual fire as possible. Later, investigators determined that the fire began in a hotel deli before it opened for business on November 21. The ignition source was an electrical ground fault inside a wall soffit that powered a refrigeration compressor for a pie case. The vibration of the compressor caused the wires to rub together and then arc due to the friction, resulting in the deli's display cabinet bursting into flames. The pie case was next to a deli bus station where the staff stored plastic utensils and paper napkins. Once the open flaming of the bus station took place, the plastic and paper products and combustible materials such as wood, ceiling tile adhesive, and foam plastic padding of chairs and booths rapidly fueled the fire. The resulting "flashover" contributed to the dense smoke that raced up the tower.

Within six minutes, a fireball raced into the casino area, engulfing it in flames. Ten people in the casino were unable to escape and burned to death.

Although Sully and Frankie had planned to go to dinner and a Las Vegas show to celebrate their anniversary, they were just grateful to be alive. They opted to attend a Billy Graham crusade instead. Reverend Graham was on-site during rescue operations and ministered to many of the survivors of the deadly fire.

All victims or their families filed negligent suits against the MGM Grand Hotel except Sully and his wife. As a result, they were awarded a complimentary luxury suite for life after the hotel was restored and reopened under a new name: Bally's Las Vegas. They did go back once and were given a tour of the new hotel's state-of-the-art fire and safety features. Had these features been in place on November 21, 1980, there may not have been any loss of life.

After surviving one of the worst hotel fires in history, Frankie passed away two years later. Sully was torn apart and died soon after of a broken heart.

The Story Behind the Story

My husband and I were on a Delta Queen cruise on the Mississippi River many years ago. There was an elderly couple who were also on the cruise assigned to our dinner table. We were all spellbound by the gentleman's story about their rescue from the fire at the MGM Grand hotel in Las Vegas. The story stuck with me, and I wondered if I could tell it as a short story. I imagined what was said as he and his wife feared for their lives, and I researched how the fire started and why so many things went wrong in such a state-of-the-art hotel.

Demanding, Disappointing, and Maybe Even Delusional

Sometimes, the things we love doing the most can feel like all of these—I know it's true of writing. Putting words on paper can be downright exasperating. You have to start somewhere, and often, that's the hardest part. You can't always wait for or expect inspiration to come along to ease the pain of staring at a blank page. Ironically, inspiration can be the most demanding aspect of writing—because it won't leave you alone. You have this fantastic idea or vision that seems to have come out of nowhere, yet you still struggle to find the right words.

Then there are the times when you get things right, and your work is finally published. It's not the end, however. You have to get noticed, and you can easily fall into the lap of disappointment when you realize how difficult this is. While most of your friends and family may support you, you must get beyond them to make a difference. They, too, disappoint by not reading what you've written or providing any feedback. There is only one remedy: keep writing, baring your soul, and stop depending on others for satisfaction.

For the Love of Money

Jodi began working at the Painted Stallion Bar & Grill downtown a few weeks after she broke off her engagement with Kyle. She had already become friends with Jill, the waitress training her. One evening, when things were slow, Jill ushered Jodi to an empty table in the back corner.

"I have a favor to ask," said Jill.

"By all means." Jodi wondered if this had something to do with work.

"My boyfriend Vince has gotten himself in trouble. He's in jail awaiting trial."

"What did he do?"

"Nothing. Someone falsely accused Vince of dealing drugs, although he claims they were planted on him. I'm sure he'll be acquitted of all charges."

"So, what does this have to do with me?"

"Before he was arrested, Vince asked me to keep some cash he had been saving so we could get married and buy a house. I'm afraid the authorities will search my apartment for something they can hang on Vince, and they'd probably think the money was from selling drugs."

"I see what you mean," said Jodi, still not understanding what Jill wanted from her.

"Anyway, I know I could trust you to hold onto the money until Vince gets this mess straightened out."

"Oh, I don't know about that." Jodi was taken aback.

"It's just for a short while," Jill pleaded. "I'm not asking you to do anything wrong. It took Vince a long time to save that money, and I'm just trying to ensure it doesn't disappear because it looks suspicious."

"Well, I guess it would be ok." Jodi finally gave in to Jill.

Jill slipped a zipper bank deposit bag into Jodi's large satchel purse the next day. When Jodi got home, she counted the money, astonished that the amount was almost seventy thousand dollars. Jodi had never seen that much cash in all her life.

Jodi stuffed the money bag in one of her riding boots, then placed the pair back inside a large shoe box she kept on the shelf above the clothes rack. No one would look there, she thought.

Jodi soon forgot about the secret stash; even Jill never mentioned it. A few weeks later, Jodi's car needed repair, but she didn't have enough money to fix it, so she borrowed some cash hidden in the boot, which Jodi was sure she could pay back before anyone knew it was missing. Before long, Jodi found it easy to take a few dollars here and there to pay for whatever caught her attention: a new dress, a nice meal at a restaurant, and even some expensive jewelry. She even booked a cruise for herself and a friend to the Bahamas.

"Where are you getting the money to pay for the trip?" asked Jill when Jodi showed up for work one evening.

"I put it on my credit card," said Jodi.

"Don't lie to me, Jodi. Are you spending Vince's money?"

"Ok, I shouldn't have done it. I plan to pay every penny back."

"With what? You're a waitress. If Vince gets wind of this, he'll be furious."

"Please don't tell him. I promise I'll figure out something and even cancel the cruise."

"Well, you better. That's all I can say," said Jill.

Two days later, Jodi received a note in her mailbox demanding that she meet with two of Vince's friends to discuss how she would repay the missing money. The instructions gave her the time, date, and address.

Nervous about meeting strangers at an unfamiliar location, Jodi decided to see if her former fiancé, Kyle, would accompany her. On the scheduled meeting date, she drove to the house where Kyle and his two roommates lived.

"Is Kyle here?" Jodi asked when Jim answered her knock.

"Let me get him. Do you want to come inside?"

"No, I'll wait out here." Jodi sat on the porch swing.

Kyle's other roommate, Greg, stuck his head out the door to say hello.

Kyle was surprised to see Jodi, who asked him to sit beside her as she told him why she had come to see him.

"This sounds serious, Jodi. You've gotten yourself in big trouble, and I don't think you should meet up with these guys."

"Neither do I, but what else can I do but talk to them? I'm sure it will be ok if you go with me." Jodi had always felt safe with Kyle, who was tall and muscular from working out regularly in the gym.

Jodi and Kyle drove away in Jodi's car to the address given in the instructions. They parked the car in front of a rundown house in an old neighborhood, and a baldheaded guy opened the door as they walked up the front steps.

"Who's this?" the guy asked Jodi as a second man appeared in the dimly lit hallway.

"Kyle is a friend of mine. I asked him to come with me." Jodi smiled nervously.

"We're not meeting here," said the baldheaded man whose arms were twice as big as Kyle's. "Pete here will follow me in your car since we're going to a remote area where our boss lives."

"Can't we just settle this here?" asked Kyle.

"Look, man, this doesn't concern you, so just do what we say."

The sun was already beginning to set as they pulled off the main road and parked both cars. Pete opened the back door of Jodi's car and motioned for them to get out.

"Keep walking. Stay behind her," the baldheaded man ordered Kyle as they made their way through the trees and brush.

Jodi flinched as a muffled shot rang behind her. She turned as Kyle collapsed to the ground after being hit in the back of his head with a .22LR pistol. Jodi panicked and began to run, but Pete was close enough to deliver a second bullet that entered her skull and overcame her. She fell just a few feet from Kyle.

After not hearing from them for several days, Jodi and Kyle's families began worrying. Jodi's mother went on local TV to plead for anyone with information to come forward. Kyle's roommates were the last people, aside from their assassins, to see them alive. In their discussions with the detectives on the case, Greg and Jim revealed that Jodi and Kyle left together in Jodi's car shortly after they talked on the front porch for about twenty minutes. They also said Jodi seemed upset about something, but they had not overheard her conversation with Kyle.

A week later, Jodi's car was found parked on a street where mainly renters lived in shabby homes. Her parents and friends agreed that going to that part of town would have been unusual for her. Even more disturbing was that the keys were in the car, and there was no evidence of wrongdoing.

The authorities interviewed everyone who worked with Jodi at the Painted Stallion, but her friend Jill was the only person of interest. Jill, knowing it might look like she was somehow connected with the disappearance of her friend, told the detectives that she had asked Jodi to keep some money for her since there had been several break-ins at her apartment complex. The cops weren't buying her story, so they made a deal with her to tell them where the money came from and any information that she could offer to help them find the missing couple.

A few days later, a man pulled off the side of the road to let his dog out for a run. The dog ran up into the woods and began barking. When the dog didn't obey his command, the man went after him. To his horror, the dog was hovering over two badly decomposing bodies. The man gagged before returning to his car to contact the county sheriff.

Although it seemed likely that Vince ordered a hit on Jodi for ripping him off, it was clear he wasn't the one who shot the victims since he was in jail when the killings occurred. There wasn't any evidence to press charges against him, nor were the baldheaded man and his accomplice, Pete, ever discovered.

Jodi's mother never got over her loss. Each evening, she would open her Bible, placing her finger on the one verse that explained her daughter's death above all else: "For the love of money is the root for all kinds of evil." (1 Timothy 6:10)

The Story Behind the Story

This story was based on a similar incident involving a friend of mine many years ago. Although many of the elements are fictional, especially the actual thoughts and dialog of the participants, the eeriness of this tragic event continues to haunt me. The story reflects how easily we can be persuaded to do things we would never usually agree to. This story was awarded First Place in the 2024 Short Stories and Poems by Texas Authors contest.

THE FORGOTTEN SIBLING

The most overlooked form of grief is that of the forgotten sibling. It happens all too often when a family loses a child, and the surviving siblings must navigate the waters of grief on their own. It's not intentional. No one would argue that "burying a child is life's darkest assignment." The parents are too consumed with their loss to realize that they're not the only ones who are suffering. And so, the descent into the dark world of despair begins for the siblings left behind. Some overcome it, some die because of it, and others—well, I think others like me just become writers. We write our way out of the messy life we were handed.

When I read the full version of my *Kirkus Review* the other day, I was taken aback a bit. How could this reviewer do such a thing? They almost totally ignored my protagonist, Holly, in favor of her parents. They got all the attention. Did this ever sound familiar to me? Did the reviewer read my book? If so, how did he (I'm convinced the reviewer was a male) not hear Holly's heart shatter every time the page was turned? After I thought about it, I realized the reviewer picked up on exactly how I wrote the story. Holly was the forgotten sibling. Even the reviewer dismissed her as "angry and forlorn" rather than a child desperate for the love and comfort she sought from her parents following her brother's death. Perhaps this is what the reviewer meant by the "selfishness of grief." Even the forgotten sibling owns some of that. But, oh—what a gift it is for the writer! (the next best thing to having a dysfunctional family to write about).

KILLING GRANDMA

There was a virus going around, and almost everyone was scared. The scared regarded the unscared as a menace to society for not strictly following the guidelines health officials had established to prevent its spread. And the unscared bashed the scared for overreacting and spreading fear. Neither side disputed the fact that there was a virus and that people were dying from it. Although the virus was sweeping across the world at an alarming rate, the death toll was less than some expected. Even so, the scared demanded more rules to keep everyone safe, and the unscared grew defiant against obeying them. The government ordered schools and businesses to shut down. Worshipers could no longer congregate in churches. People worldwide hunkered down in their homes, allowed only to shop for food and other necessities. The politicians bickered among themselves over how to fix all the problems created by the virus. As fear spread like wildfire, the people lost more and more control over their lives. The scared and unscared both agreed that Grandma was the most vulnerable among them. And no one wanted Grandma to fall prey to a deadly virus.

Kelly and her twin brother Kyle loved spending time with their Grandma Emma. She would sit with them on the front porch swing. Sometimes, they sang songs, and she would read to them other times. When Kelly and Kyle visited, Grandma always served freshly baked cookies and a pitcher of lemonade. But the best time of all was when they got to stay overnight. On summer evenings, Grandma would spread a quilt on the ground so she and the twins would lie on their backs and gaze at the stars. Laura Otis dreaded telling her children they could no longer visit Grandma.

"Why?" asked Kelly.

"There's a virus that's making people sick. We have to protect Grandma since she's older than us."

"Grandma never gets sick," said Kyle.

"And we don't want her to," said Laura. "That's why we have to stay away from all people."

"But we're people," said Kelly. "Why should we be afraid of people?"

"If we caught the virus from someone, we might pass it on to Grandma," said Laura.

"But we're not sick," said Kelly. "Why can't we go see her?"

"We could have the germs and not know it," said Laura. "We have to make sure Grandma is safe."

Grandma Emma was just as disappointed as her grandchildren when she learned they could not be together. Talking on the phone was not the same as hugging one another. And besides, Grandma couldn't hear very well. Even though Grandma still drove, her daughter prohibited her from going anywhere, especially to the store. No need to, Laura had told her. When dropping off a bag of groceries for her mother, Laura would set them on the front porch and then leave. Grandma was appalled that her daughter wouldn't step foot inside her home.

"It's for your safety," Laura insisted. "We have to do social distancing to save lives."

Kelly and Kyle made cards for Grandma. They drew pictures of themselves on the front and wrote cheery notes inside. Each time Grandma opened a bag of groceries, she would find a card. And while she loved the cards, they made her miss her grandchildren even more. The days and weeks passed slowly. Every day was like the one before. Grandma had lived by herself since her husband had died seven years ago from lung cancer. She had never been as alone, however, as she was now. Grandma enjoyed family gatherings and always went to church on Sundays. She was a member of a knitting group and a book club, and she also liked having friends over for tea and mahjong. Now, no one dropped by, other than Laura, with a bag of groceries. The mail carrier used to take a break and chat with her if she was sitting on her porch swing. But not anymore. Everyone was afraid of everyone. And now they were wearing silly masks. It felt like even the birds were keeping their distance.

Kelly and Kyle also found their lives impacted by the virus. They couldn't play with their friends. They couldn't go to the park, the movie theatre, or the library. And although they had regularly complained about going to school, they now wished they were in the classroom. But most of all, they missed seeing Grandma. The economic loss due to the virus was devastating. Many workers lost their jobs. The government poured trillions of dollars on a raging fire that continued to burn. The world was gloomy, and no one knew how to improve it. Grandma had always trusted doctors' opinions, but more and more, she was unsure who to believe. Some said the virus was deadlier than the flu, and others said it was more like a bad cold. Having lived for a long time, Grandma knew that fear, not the virus, posed the highest risk to humanity.

Laura called on Grandma Emma's birthday to say she was bringing the twins to see her. Grandma could hardly wait for them to get there. She went to the mirror and looked at herself. Her hair was as unkempt as a monkey's. Grandma could not go to her weekly hair appointment for over a month. She smoothed her hair with her hands and put on some fresh lipstick. The phone rang as she sat down to wait for her grandchildren to arrive.

"Mom, we're here," said Laura when Grandma answered.

"I didn't hear the doorbell," said Grandma.

"No, we're outside. Raise the blinds, and you'll see us."

"You're not coming inside?"

"Mom, you know we can't do that. Look outside, please. Kelly and Kyle can't wait to see you."

Grandma hung up the phone and sighed as she approached the window and raised the blinds. Kelly and Kyle were standing on the sidewalk. They started jumping up and down and waving their hands when they saw Grandma staring out the window. Grandma waved back at them and blew them a kiss. Tears rolled down her eyes when the twins held up the giant birthday card they had made for her. She motioned for them to come up on the porch. Grandma placed both her hands against the glass window. Each twin pressed one of their hands over one of hers as if touching through the glass. It was a beautiful moment that none of them would ever forget.

"Let's go," said Laura.

Kelly and Kyle reluctantly walked back to the car with their mother.

"How much longer before we can go inside to visit?" asked Kelly.

"I don't know," said Laura. "The most important thing is keeping Grandma safe."

"By living in a bubble?" asked Kyle.

"It won't be this way forever," said Laura.

"I don't want Grandma to live in a bubble." Kelly began to cry.

Grandma remained at the window until she could no longer see the rear wheels of Laura's car. She sat on the sofa and looked through the photo albums she had piled on the coffee table earlier that day. Grandma smiled as memories of weddings, picnics, and birthdays flashed before her eyes. The albums were a storybook of her whole life. Everything that made her life worthwhile was taken away by those who sought to protect her. Were all the measures put in place to stop the virus worth it, Grandma wondered? No one living during these tumultuous times would live long enough to know the truth. Perhaps historians, centuries from now, would deem this the Age of Unreason.

That night, Grandma Emma laid down and died of a broken heart.

The Story Behind the Story

This story is a fictional account of how many felt during the Pandemic of 2020-2021. History will remember the division among those who lived through this time of fear and uncertainty for many years.

Storyteller or Liar?

When I was growing up, if someone called you a storyteller, it meant you were a liar. There may be some truth in that. Fiction, after all, is made-up tales created by the imagination or a distortion of facts. Storytelling is as old as time—it was invented long before anything was written down. Some of the most notable storytellers across the ages include the Greek fabulist Aesop and Geoffrey Chaucer, whose Middle English *Canterbury Tales* depict a group of traveling pilgrims who try to outdo each other in a storytelling contest. Let's not forget the parables of Jesus in the New Testament or Abraham Lincoln's humorous anecdotes. The list is endless.

My debut as a storyteller was in the second grade. I shamelessly began telling a few close friends about the nasty fight between my parents the night before. My father had been drinking heavily, and my mother was madder than a wet hen about it. Before long, more classmates gathered around my desk as I continued to embellish the details. Some swore they would run away if anything like that happened to their families. Yep, I had everyone's attention, including my teacher's. Word got back to my parents that I was a tattletale. I was in big trouble.

Honestly, I like to think that I came by my storytelling ability through my father, also known as a storyteller. Most of his stories involved humor, though he revealed later in life some dark moments he experienced in World War II. Although others and I have passed on some of his stories, many are lost forever. I regret not having recorded more of them. I think of storytelling as "audible writing." The best stories make an audience cry, laugh, or be scared to death. Others reveal human nature or serve as moral lessons. Our social identity is embedded in the stories we tell. Traditions and history are passed down from one generation to another through stories shared at family gatherings. Without stories, who are we?

Lost Boy of Sudan

When my neighbor Sherry asked me to come over, I didn't suspect she had more on her mind than sitting by the swimming pool and having a glass of wine. It was late September; the leaves had begun to change colors, and the temperature was mild. Sharon wasted no time with small talk.

"I wonder if you could help me out?" Sherry began. "I've agreed to host two lost boys in my home."

"Lost boys?" I asked. "How old are they, and where are their parents?"

"First, let me explain. I'm talking about two boys from southern Sudan who recently came to the United States with the help of the International Rescue Committee. There were about 20,000 young boys who fled to Ethiopia following the brutal murder of their families and the destruction of their villages."

"But didn't that take place a while back?" I asked.

"Yes, during the civil war of 1987. Most of the boys were only six or seven years old. They were working in the fields, tending cattle when the slaughter occurred. They could hear the horrific screams of their family members and knew they had to flee. During the next few months and years, they walked more than a thousand miles to escape death or induction into the Northern Army. Those were their choices. Half of the boys died before reaching the Kakuma refugee camp in Kenya."

"I can't imagine what that would be like," I said. "Aren't these boys grown now?"

"Yes, and no. The savage war had stolen the young boys' childhoods and forced them to parent themselves in a way few of us can imagine. The workers in the camp began referring to them as the 'Lost Boys,' like the children's story of the orphaned boys led by Peter Pan in Never Land. Although they were young men in their early twenties by then, like Peter Pan, they had never grown up.

"So, what is it you want me to do?" I hoped Sherry was not suggesting that I also host a Lost Boy. My husband Robert would never agree to it, and I wasn't sure if I had what it takes to host someone.

"The boys learned English in the refugee camp but little else. The things we take for granted, such as drawing water from a faucet, flushing a toilet, or turning on a light switch, are foreign to them. One of the boys I'm hosting has been hired by Radio Shack to help receive and shelve supplies since he's more advanced in English. Since you do the neighborhood newsletter, I thought you could post an ad for the other boy. Or ask anyone you know if they could help him find work that doesn't require much skill or knowledge. His name is Peter, a common name given to many of the Lost Boys."

"I would be glad to do that. In the meantime, perhaps I could hire Peter to help me weed my flower beds. They are pretty ragged due to my neglect."

"You understand that you will have to show him everything you want him to do?" asked Sherry. "Although he worked in the fields of Sudan, he has no clue about flower beds. He might just as well mistake your roses or azaleas for a weed."

"I will work alongside him. Send Peter over at ten o'clock tomorrow morning. I will be out front waiting for him."

"Thank you so much," said Sherry.

"Well, I can't believe you are doing this. I hope all goes well."

The next morning, I went outside to determine where to start weeding. At precisely ten o'clock, I saw a tall, thin man walking up the driveway. I had not expected him to be taller than me. His skin was as dark as coal and very shiny. Peter did not smile, and he looked at me with uncertainty.

"Hello, Peter," I greeted him.

"Hello, Mrs., I am here to work."

"Please call me Patricia."

"Yes, Pa . . . tri . . ."

"Or you can call me Pat if that is easier. Let's sit on the sidewalk so I can show you what to do."

Peter and I sat down with our knees bent and our legs folded beneath us. I gave him a garden spade and showed him how to pull up weeds.

"Why do you do this?" asked Peter.

"Weeds choke the garden. They rob plants of water, food, sunshine, and space. Weeds can harm the plants we eat and those we enjoy looking at."

"But why grow plants you do not eat?"

"That's a good question, Peter. But here, we like to have beautiful plants to look at."

"I ate any plant I saw when I was hungry."

"Not every plant is good to eat and can make you sick. Oh, but look, the deer have eaten some of my shrubs." I sighed upon seeing how much damage they had done to my azaleas.

Peter grew very quiet.

"Is something wrong?" I asked.

"Will the deer eat me?" Peter spoke like a child.

"Why would you think that? Of course not!"

"When the other boys in the fields and I fled to escape the soldiers as they murdered our families, we had nothing but the clothes on our backs. We had little to eat, mainly berries and leaves. We sometimes ate soft mud if there was no river water to drink. Villagers along the way offered us food, which largely kept us alive. We were afraid to sleep, no matter how tired we were. We kept walking, hiding in the bushes if we heard anyone. Eventually, we met up with more boys who had endured the same fate. The older boys became our leaders, although most were only twelve or thirteen."

"I don't think I would have lasted very long under those conditions," I said.

"We suffered hunger and constant danger. Our biggest threats were militia gunfire and being eaten alive by lions or leopards as we ran across sub-Saharan Africa in search of safety. Often, we had to dive into the river to escape the soldiers and predators. The river, too, became a watery grave for those who couldn't swim or were attacked by crocodiles."

"I can't even imagine what your life must have been like, Peter."

A silence fell over us. There was nothing I could think of to say that could erase the pain this young man would carry with him for the rest of his life. I now understood how Peter, a grown man with the innocence of a child, was afraid of encountering the deer that grazed in my garden beds.

"I try not to let my past make me afraid of things," Peter stated.

"You do not have to be afraid of the deer; they mainly eat plants. And if you came across a deer, they would flee faster than you could blink your eyes."

As Peter and I pulled weeds, I thought about how children in all societies are nurtured by their parents, family, and community and by the stories, legends, and myths passed down from generation to generation.

The lessons they learn teach them values and essential skills for overcoming life's difficulties. Without these fundamental teachings, the Lost Boys relied entirely on the strongest instinct of all—survival.

Around noon, I brought out some small plates with fruit, cheese, and crackers for Peter and me. Peter especially liked the lemonade I had made. After lunch, I suggested we work on another project. Peter seemed grateful not to have to pull any more weeds.

We're going to paint my picket fence," I said. "The color is fading and needs a touch-up."

We went to the backyard. I opened the can of bluish-green paint and gave Peter a brush. I was sure he had never painted a fence before.

"Let me show you," I said as I dipped my brush into the can. Peter watched as I painted two slats. "Now you try."

Peter carefully applied the paint on several slats. He looked at me and said, "You can go away now. I can do this."

I smiled at Peter and put down my paintbrush. I felt sure Peter would be just fine, no matter what he did in the coming months and years.

Most Lost Boys in America became U.S. citizens and graduated from college. Many returned to their former homes in Sudan, only to find that a new war had broken out.

I still think of Peter and hope he is safe wherever he is.

The Story Behind the Story

This story is entirely accurate. It was a great learning experience for me. What seemed like essential matters in my world were trivial compared to Peter's life experience. But still, we found a way to bond, and that's what matters the most.

"Lost Boy of Sudan" received an award in 2024 from the Texas Authors Institute's annual short story contest.

Some Things Still Matter

January 27 marks the anniversary each year of the liberation of Auschwitz. Although that event was a long time ago, it still matters. A neighbor of ours, when we lived in Atlanta, was one of the survivors of the death camp. Murray Lynne was born in Hungary in 1930. He was the oldest of his parents' four boys. In 1942, a fascist group similar to Germany's Nazi party showed up at his home and took away his father. The fascists executed Murray's father along with fifteen other Jewish leaders in his community. Later that night, one of the fascists returned to Murray's home and raped his mother. Two weeks after that, the fascist group rounded up Murray's mother and her four sons and put them in a cattle car headed for Auschwitz. For Murray's mother and his three younger brothers, this meant immediate death upon arrival in the gas chamber. Murray, on the advice from another prisoner, lied about his age, claiming he was sixteen rather than fourteen—a lie which marked him for labor rather than the gas chamber.

Each time Murray gives a speech, he writes out what he wants to say on a yellow tablet. When his presentation is finished, he crumples the yellow pages and throws them away. Murray does this because he wants what he says to remain fresh and perhaps even tender each time he tells it. Murray's story made a lasting impression on me. He shares it because he knows that what happened to more than six million Jews in the 1940s still matters.

Love is Blue

"I can't wait for tonight," said Kate to her best friends, Sarah and Laura.

"Me either," said Sarah. "I can't believe Madam Joubert asked the entire orchestra to come to our wine tasting."

"Too bad they can't come," said Laura.

"Yes, but just think," said Sarah, "M. Mauriat invited the members of the French Club to come backstage after their performance."

"I don't know what to wear," said Kate, who hoped to stand out in the crowd. Paul Mauriat was her favorite composer, so meeting him in person was overwhelming.

The girls spent the afternoon trying on different outfits and fixing their hair. The French Club's wine tasting, hosted by their professor, Madam Joubert, began at five-thirty before the concert. And while it met all their expectations for a lovely evening, they were more enthused about hearing "Love is Blue" live in the college auditorium instead of on the radio or their record player.

When the curtains opened, the audience gasped with pleasure as the French conductor began by playing the hit song's familiar harpsichord himself. Soon, the auditorium swelled with the brilliant sounds of violins, saxophones, the tambourine, and other instruments.

The three friends got up and went backstage once the last strains of "Love is Blue" ended, signaling the concert's close.

They looked all around for M. Mauriat until one of the violinists told them the conductor had slipped out the back door. Disappointed, they began chatting with the various musicians. About half were French, and the rest were from New York City. One of them invited them to the party they were having at their hotel. Surly, their idol would be there. The room where the party was held was too small to accommodate all the people that had been invited. It bothered Kate, Sarah, and Laura that a few girls in the room were not French Club members.

"We can move the party to my house," said Kate. "It's not far from here."

Kate and Sarah lived in a wood-frame house with their other roommate, Beth, who had not attended the concert. Kate called Beth to let her know what to expect.

"Are you drunk?" asked Beth. "I don't believe you."

"Well, don't say I didn't warn you."

Everyone at the party followed Kate onto the parking lot. As they walked toward Lincoln Street, Kate saw M. Mauriat walking in their direction. One of the violinists ran ahead of the group to let the conductor know what they were doing. M. Mauriat came up to Kate, who was almost breathless from excitement.

"Will you join us?" Kate asked shyly as M. Mauriat took her hand, bowed slightly, and kissed it. Kate thought she might faint as she gazed into his grayish-green eyes.

"Je regrette, Mademoiselle. Mais, s'il vous plait, avez un bon temps. Thank you for coming to my concert."

"We loved it," said Kate, sorry he had not accepted her invitation.

By the time the group arrived at Kate and Sarah's house, most of the girls who were not members of the French Club had gone away. Kate estimated that about twenty-five musicians, mostly in their early twenties, were now in her house. They had brought several bottles of wine to add to the small number in Kate's refrigerator. Soon, the house was filled with smoke from the cigarettes and weed her guests lit as they wandered about the kitchen and living room. Some took turns playing the out-of-tune piano owned by the landlord who lived nearby.

Kate's bedroom was large enough to serve as an extra sitting area, with a row of windows that let in abundant light. Several musicians followed her there when she went to turn on the stereo, and one of the sax players sat on the floor next to her.

"I'm Dennis," said the bearded, dark-haired New Yorker. "How come you're here?"

"This is where I live." Kate was confused by his question.

"I've been listening to you talk to the others. This place doesn't seem right for you."

"I'm not sure what you mean." Kate twisted a strand of hair with her fingers.

"Here you are in this small college town. You're more sophisticated than that. Don't you want to see the world, to find what's out there just waiting for you?"

"Well, I have been to Paris and went to school there the summer after my freshman year."

"Most likely, that's why you come across a cut above your friends."

"Thank you, but I'm happy where I am."

"Are you?"

"And how happy are you?" Kate tossed the question back to Dennis.

"About the same as you, I suppose."

"What is your life like?" asked Kate.

"Well, for one, I travel most of my time. It's so special to be invited to someone's home; we never get to meet the people who come to hear us play. We wrap up the evening with a joint and wine or beer when our concert ends. Then we go to bed. We're usually back on the bus around six in the morning."

"Where all do you perform?"

"All over the place, usually in small college towns like this one. They're easier to book since large venues are booked far in advance and must conform to more rigid requirements. But, there's nothing like a smaller crowd that adores you."

"Getting to hear and see Paul Mauriat and his orchestra play 'Love is Blue' is a dream come true."

"What is it you like about that particular piece?"

"It is music 'pour faire l'amour.'"

"Ah, you want to make love when you hear it?" Dennis grinned when Kate blushed.

"Remind me not to speak French anymore tonight."

"It's getting late, and we should head back to the hotel. Tomorrow will come soon enough."

Kate and her roommates said goodbye to the orchestra members and shooed everyone else away. Beth wished she had gone to the concert, and Kate and Sarah still felt high from the night's unexpected twist.

"Is it true that Paul Mauriat kissed your hand?" asked Beth.

"He did! His eyes were mesmerizing, and his touch was as gentle as a drop of rain. M. Mauriat wore a pale blue tuxedo that made his eyes look more blue than green, and his mustache was neatly trimmed. You would have loved the concert; I can't fully describe it."

Sarah awoke the following morning when she heard Kate moving two suitcases from her bedroom to the front door.

"What are you doing?" she asked.

"I'm leaving," said Kate.

"But, what about school? What brought this on?" Sarah asked.

"It was something Dennis, the sax player, pointed out when he said I should be in New York, not here."

"And you believe him? You're smarter than that. Sounds like a pickup line to me."

"It wasn't. Dennis never made any moves like you're suggesting. How will I ever know if I don't bother to find out what he said is true? I'm taking a bus to Dallas and then flying to Denver." Kate's parents had recently moved to Colorado, so it seemed practical to go there first. Besides, she needed money, and convincing them to help her would be easier in person.

"Well, Denver isn't like New York."

"It's my starting point. I want to get out of here for a while. I may be back, and then again, I may not."

"I can't imagine what your parents are going to think. Mine would disown me if I did something like this."

"I'm willing to take the risk," said Kate, tired of arguing.

"You're not going to do something stupid and try to hook up with the orchestra, are you? Dennis was handsome enough to impress you, but you know nothing about him."

"Please don't lecture me; I know what I'm doing."

"If I had a car, I'd drive you to the bus station."

"That's ok. Laura will be by soon to take me."

Kate woke Beth so she could say goodbye. The roommates had enough time to share coffee before Laura arrived.

"I can't believe you're doing this," said Beth. "But I suppose it shouldn't surprise me. You always have enough guts to do the craziest things."

Laura parked her car and got out to help Kate load her luggage in the back seat.

"You're sure about this?" she asked.

"Why is everyone doubting me?" Kate whined.

"Well, it is a bit sudden. You go to a concert, talk to one of the musicians, and then change your life's plan overnight."

"Just take me to the bus station, please. I can't explain it."

"At your service." Laura didn't say another word the rest of the way.

Laura and Kate got out of the car and carried Kate's bags to the ticket counter. After purchasing her ticket, Kate hugged her friend and said goodbye.

The bus pulled up, and after a few passengers got off, the porter helped Kate, and a middle-aged couple put their luggage in the baggage compartment.

As Kate started up the steps of the bus, she turned her head toward the parking lot, but Laura had already driven away. She climbed the last step and entered the bus. It was too late to change her mind. She walked down the aisle, still hearing the haunting melody of "Love is Blue" in her head, to an empty seat and sat down, wondering where life was taking her as the bus pulled from the station.

The Story Behind the Story

This story was mostly true. The orchestra came to my home, and M. Mauriat kissed my hand. And although I didn't run away from where I was, I often wondered if I made the right decision. Choices are always complicated, but rather than regretting them, we should accept the path we took and make the most of it.

What's in a Name?

According to Shakespeare, "That which we call a rose by any other name would smell as sweet." (*Romeo and Juliet*) Or would it? As a writer, I know how important it is to find the correct title. It may be the most critical marketing decision you'll have to make. I like metaphoric titles such as *Gone with the Wind* and *Far from the Madding Crowd*. One of the most successful metaphoric titles was *Chicken Soup for the Soul*.

I borrowed the title of my novel from the last line of a poem by Edna St. Vincent Millay. *The Eyes of the Doe* is a metaphor for my life experience.

Some titles come from Scripture. *East of Eden, Stranger in a Strange Land*, and *The Little Foxes* are good examples.

Then, there are symbolic titles. *Fahrenheit 451* (the temperature at which book paper catches fire) warns against state-run censorship. *To Kill a Mockingbird* symbolizes the sin of harming the innocent.

I love it when someone asks me where I got the title of my book. That means it got their attention—hopefully enough to make them want to read cover to cover.

Map Maker

James Robert Taylor's life was about to change. He had never been anywhere other than the East Texas community where he was born. But he was also smart and graduated high school when he was only sixteen. His father was a lawyer who owned a land and title plant and hoped his son would follow in his footsteps. Jim, as he was called, enrolled in a small college nearby, but he was immature and didn't like to study. Eventually, he dropped out of school and went back home. His father began teaching him everything there was to know about running an abstract title plant, including how to survey land and draw maps.

Once World War II was underway, all men between eighteen and sixty-four were required to register for military service. Jim voluntarily enlisted in the U.S. Army, happy to learn that due to his map-making skills, he was assigned as a Technical Sergeant, and his deployment overseas would be delayed while he trained in the States.

Eventually, Jim was deployed to New Guinea, where he served in the Sixth Army under Lt. General Walter Krueger. The Pentagon was planning an invasion of Luzon, the largest island in the Philippines. At three o'clock each afternoon, Jim would disappear to the Map Room adjacent to Army Headquarters to work on the top-secret maps detailing the military installations that agents and Pilipino guerrillas gathered daily for the invasion.

After slipping through the Finance Department, where the payroll cash was kept, the guards would lift a tarp that opened to the Six Army Headquarters Situation Room. From there, other guards opened the door to the Map Room, where Jim would work solo for two to three hours updating the maps for the invasion. He was involved in other Army intelligence matters the rest of the time.

The temperature in New Guinea was often as high as 115 degrees Fahrenheit. Despite the heat, General Krueger had ordered all his soldiers to keep their collars and sleeves buttoned to prevent bites from poisonous insects, which could be just as lethal as the enemy's weapons. One day,

Major Charles A. Willoughby, General Douglas MacArthur's Chief of Intelligence, stopped by to look at the maps. He noticed Jim was sweating profusely despite his efforts to conceal his discomfort. The major implored Lt. General Krueger to allow Jim to strip down while working on the maps as long as no one else was in the room.

There was a big meeting after it was determined that the invasion of the Philippines would not take place at Mindanao, the southernmost of its large islands, but at Leyte in the central Philippines instead. The meeting included General MacArthur, Lt. General Krueger, Vice Admiral Thomas C. Kinkaid of the U.S. Seventh Fleet, General George C. Kenney of the U.S. Fifth Army Air Force, two U.S. Senators, and three U.S. House Representatives. Jim had been told to remain quiet and not repeat anything he heard if anyone entered the Situation Room that adjoined the Map Room.

General MacArthur was eager to show off the maps prepared for the invasion, not knowing that Jim was in the next room. Jim froze as the general threw open the huge doors, expecting a room full of laughter when the group saw him in his underwear. Instead, everyone was as quiet as a church mouse. General MacArthur jumped in front of the group, proclaiming, "This is a uniform that I have authorized for this young soldier only when he is working in the Top-Secret Map Room in the Southwest Pacific."

General MacArthur then looked directly at Jim and said," You are not a field grade officer, so I must ask you to leave." A bit embarrassed, Jim quickly gathered his clipboard, uniform, shoes, and gun.

As he left the room, one of the Congressmen stopped Jim and asked if he could shake his hand. "Young man, where are you from?"

"Texas," replied Jim, struggling to shake hands while carrying his belongings.

"Oh, shoot," said the disappointed Representative who had hoped for a story and photo opportunity to share with his constituents back home.

In July 1944, General Douglas MacArthur and Admiral Chester Nimitz flew to Hawaii to meet with President Roosevelt to discuss the strategy for invading the South Pacific Islands under Japanese control. General MacArthur was determined to restore the honor of himself and the American people from the time President Roosevelt ordered him, his family, and staff to leave the Philippines because the Japanese had surrounded them and would likely try to assassinate the general. On the other hand, Admiral Nimitz was focused on leapfrogging the smaller islands north of the Mid-Pacific.

Now that the Philippine invasion point was officially changed from Mindanao to Leyte, Jim had to rush to make a new map since the planned invasion was less than a month away. Out of the clear blue sky, Jim spotted a Magnolia Petroleum Company roadmap of Leyte, which saved the day. He used this map and the aerial photos the Fifth Army Air Force provided to overlay the coordinates the Sixth Army would use for the invasion. Later, on September 24, Navy pilots under Admiral Marc Mitscher bombed the central Philippines and conducted photographic surveillance around Leyte.

On October 13, 1944, the convoy carrying troops, supplies, and equipment left Hollandia in New Guinea for the Gulf of Leyte. It would take ten days to reach their destination. Vice Admiral Thomas C. Kinkaid took over as the fleet commander of the amphibious command ship *USS Wasatch* on October 14. Lt. General Walter Krueger was also aboard. Although he was only a staff sergeant, Jim and three other enlisted men from the Six Army were also on the ship headed for the Philippines.

Jim did not begin receiving enemy installations and other information by radio until the fifth day of the journey. Once, when Jim was updating his maps inside the command center of the *Wasatch*, Vice Admiral Kinkaid stopped by to see how things were going. The admiral picked up one of the maps lying on the desk.

"Where did you get this?" asked the admiral.

"I made it," said Jim. "I used aerial photos and a Magnolia Petroleum Company roadmap of Leyte."

"The Navy doesn't have a map of Leyte as good as this. Do you mind if I borrow your map for a couple of days? I want to add the Navy grid to it."

"Yes, sir." Jim nodded. There wasn't anything he could do but give the admiral the map.

A day later, Vice Admiral Kinkaid returned the map and showed Jim how to use the Navy Grid Calculator to pinpoint target positions by overlaying a template on the grids of the map. Jim's map was on a large table where five Navy officers with headphones sat as they communicated with aircraft carriers and battleships, sending the enemy targets Jim gave them to the planes in the air.

Once the *Wasatch* reached its destination on the morning of October 20, it stood offshore, serving as the nerve center for the operation underway. General Douglas MacArthur was nearby on the USS Nashville, waiting and watching as the troops landed on Leyte Island. A little later, the Navy officers on the *Wasatch* took off their headphones. Jim gave them a puzzled look.

"We're in recess," explained one of the officers. "The planes will still be flying. The war will resume in a couple of hours."

No one mentioned that General MacArthur, his key staff, the Philippine President, Sergio Osmena, and several reporters had boarded a landing craft and were heading for Red Beach on Leyte Island. Upon arrival, General MacArthur and his entourage waded ashore in knee-deep water despite enemy fire heard nearby.

General MacArthur broadcast his declaration to the Philippine people over a radio transmitter, "By the grace of Almighty God, our forces stand again on Philippine soil." Jim and the others on the *Wasatch* listened to his speech on the mess hall radio. Afterward, they returned to work. General MacArthur waded ashore the next two mornings at different beaches, repeating his promise to return to the Philippines and garnering additional photo shots of his vainglorious achievement.

Later in the late afternoon on October 20, Jim felt the Wasatch move. He feared the worst and wondered what was happening. Once again, the Navy officers removed their headphones.

"The war is over for us today," one of the officers stated. "We will return when the war resumes at eight o'clock in the morning."

The *Wasatch*, the *Nashville*, and three destroyers went out to sea to maneuver with the aircraft carriers for the safety of General Douglas MacArthur. The ships did not return until the following morning. The maneuvers continued for the next two nights. On the fourth night at sea, Jim and the other enlisted men had to sleep in the ship's hold, where food and other supplies were kept, mainly due to the large number of war correspondents on board. Jim slept on flour sacks and showered in salt water, while the reporters had beds and showered in water distilled by the ship's evaporators.

Around midnight on October 24, Lt. General Krueger's Deputy Chief of Staff, Colonel George Decker, awakened Jim and the others sleeping in the hold. The Japanese had come through the Surigao Strait and attacked the U.S. Seventh Fleet. Vice Admiral Kinkaid ordered Lt. General Krueger, the enlisted men from the Sixth Army, General MacArthur, and the war correspondents to go ashore. The admiral took over the *USS Nashville* and headed out to confront the enemy, relying heavily on PT boats armed with torpedoes to defeat the Japanese fleet. And while General MacArthur kept his promise to return to the Philippines, many were caught in the throes of war because of it. The Battle of Leyte Gulf will long be remembered as the Pacific War's Greatest Naval Battle in history.

James Robert Taylor (Tec3 Staff Sargeant) was awarded a Bronze Star for his service in the Pacific and three other medals. When the war ended, Jim returned home unscathed, other than the invisible wounds many war veterans carry with them for the rest of their lives.

The Story Behind the Story

I interviewed my father, James Robert Taylor, in 2006, a year before he died. The video I had made from the interview was lost for many years. I wanted to write his story, but without the video to rely on, it would not be the same. Seventeen years later, I decided to write what I could from memory. Soon after I began writing, I opened my desk drawer and was amazed to find the lost video. I could now capture the entire interview on paper and back it up with research. Like many World War II Veterans, my father did their part to save the world bravely, selflessly, and honorably.

"Map Maker" received an award in 2024 from the Texas Authors Institute's annual short story contest.

To the Fullest of One's Abilities

When we first learned our dog Keiko was deaf, it seemed sudden to us, almost without warning, following a slight ear infection. Her loss of hearing had been a gradual thing, so gradual that we failed to realize she had begun to ignore the doorbell or that she had stopped barking in the pre-dawn hours on trash day and no longer seemed to notice when other dogs yapped at her on our daily walks.

It took a while before we finally understood what was going on. We had come home several times and were startled when we tried to open the backdoor, only to bump it against Keiko, who was sound asleep. She would stretch out in front of the door whenever we left. She wanted to know when we came home. It was her way of adapting to a world of silence.

Although not life-threatening, Keiko's deafness had diminished her quality of life. I firmly believe that God gives all creatures the ability to overcome the meanest curves that life can throw them. Keiko was already finding ways to compensate for her limitations and continue living her life to the fullest, which I now know means "to the fullest of one's ability." In this respect, we are all created equal.

And so it was that our world became one of many gestures instead of spoken words when communicating with Keiko. And although she could no longer hear Bob when he came home from work, as soon as he kneeled beside her and gave her a tummy rub, her tail would wag. There was no guessing as to what that meant.

With any loss of ability, whether due to age or other reasons, comes the fragile realization that we are not immortal. There is a natural order to all life. Accepting things we cannot change enables us to live our lives to the fullest. I knew that despite her hearing loss, Keiko would be just fine. All I had to do was look into her eyes, and I could understand what they were saying: "Do my listening for me."

Roadblock

The early morning shade covered most of the front lawn. Liz always went out early to weed the flower beds, especially in August. She stood up and wiped her brow. Already, it was almost too hot for her to continue. She looked up the street and frowned at the number of pickups and trailers parked on both sides of the road near a house under construction.

"What do they not understand?" Liz asked herself. Parking on both sides of the street was a fire code violation since emergency trucks could barely squeeze past the lined-up vehicles. Liz thought back to the day before when her dog Renz, who had nasal cancer, began sneezing blood uncontrollably. Renz bit at Liz and her husband Hal as they attempted to round him up so they could rush him to the vet. Every minute was intense. The crowded street was nearly impassable due to open cab doors and oversized vehicles. Liz, sitting in the backseat with Renz, was as frantic as he was as she soaked up his blood with the towel she had grabbed on her way out the door.

Hal had to stop and wait for a flatbed truck driver who had pulled ahead to move out of their way. The driver took his time, sending Liz into a panic.

"This has got to stop," Liz cried, frustrated with the construction workers.

"We can't do anything about them right now," Hal replied, slowly driving down the narrow passage between the vehicles.

Renz was still sneezing blood when they arrived at the vet. Dr. Carly said he would like to keep Renz at the clinic for the rest of the day. Liz and Hal could pick him up at five o'clock.

When they turned onto their street, Liz tensed again upon seeing all the vehicles bunched up together. When Hal parked in their garage, Liz opened the car door and jumped out.

"Where are you going?" asked Hal.

"I'm going to let them have it."

"No, Liz. Come inside. You're upset, and speaking to them won't do any good."

Liz ignored Hal and marched up to the construction site. One of the workers was leaning against his car and smoking a cigarette. He rubbed it into the pavement as Liz drew nearer.

"Can you please ask everyone to park their vehicles on one side of the street?" asked Liz.

"Ma'am?"

"We had an emergency this morning. Our dog was hemorrhaging and needed medical attention."

"Oh, well, I'm sorry," said the man.

"We can't get out of here half the time as it is." Liz's voice trembled.

"I'm not in charge of where everyone parks," said the man.

"Well, somebody is. I don't want to go through this again. I need everyone to park on one side of the street. A fire truck couldn't get down here, and an ambulance would have a hard time, too."

"We'd move if there was an emergency." The man looked over his shoulder. A couple of workers had come outside to see what was going on.

"All I'm asking you is to move your vehicles to one side of the road. How hard can that be? It's all I'm asking."

"Okay, ma'am. You don't need to yell. I'll take care of it."

Liz turned and walked back to her house. Several of the workers were already moving their pickups and utility trucks. Liz breathed a sigh of relief and went inside.

Later, Liz and Hal picked Renz up and brought him home. The bleeding had stopped, and he appeared to feel better.

The day after, Renz ate a little of his breakfast. Since Hal was home, Liz decided to go outside and weed her neglected flower beds. To her disappointment, the construction workers had parked on both sides of the street again. While pulling up invasive milkweed in the front porch plot, Liz noticed a shiny black Dodge Ram turn around in the cul-de-sac right past her house. The driver slowed as he approached the house under construction. But rather than parking next to the curb, he stopped in the middle of the street. Liz watched as the driver turned off the engine and opened the cab door.

The man got out of his truck. He asked a nearby worker if the builder was around. He then started walking toward the house with a cell phone to his ear.

"Unbelievable," Liz grumbled. She walked across the lawn and stepped onto the street. "Sir?" she called out to the man. "Please don't block the street."

The man was well-dressed. He was tall with thick dark hair and a medium complexion. He had an accent that Liz couldn't place. The man turned around and stared hard at Liz.

"What?" the man asked, putting his cell in his pocket.

"Please don't block the street. No one can come or go."

"What the hell do I care?"

"Park your truck next to the curb like everyone else."

The man began walking toward Liz like a dog hunting a rabbit.

"You! Get back in your yard," the man shouted at her.

"No, you get out of the street," Liz said.

"Stupid woman," the man muttered, along with a few expletives, as he returned to his vehicle.

Liz walked back to the front porch and picked up her garden spade. The man had managed to drive up the street in hardly any time, then turned around in Liz's direction. He slowed to almost a stop in front of Liz's house.

Liz, now nervous, walked quickly toward the garage. The man rolled his truck at a snail's pace, glaring at Liz. He stopped at the driveway, blocking it.

Liz rushed to the side door next to the garage and went inside.

"Call the police," she yelled at Hal.

"What's wrong?" asked Hal.

"There's a man outside. He's blocking our drive. He threatened me."

"Threatened you?" asked Hal. He went to the front window and looked out.

"Just call the police!"

By the time the police arrived, the man had gone. Liz and Hal went outside to talk to the officers.

"So, what's going on?" asked one of the officers.

Liz told the police what had happened and described the man to them.

"Did this man do anything to harm you?" the second officer asked.

"He scared me. I was afraid he might do something."

"But he didn't, did he?"

"He blocked our driveway. And he was angry at me for telling him to move his truck."

"Well, that's not what we would call a threat," the first officer said.

"I felt threatened. The man knows where I live. I don't want him stalking me."

"I'm sorry, but there's nothing we can do."

"That's it?" asked Liz.

"I'm afraid so."

The officers left, leaving Liz feeling uncomfortable with their lack of action. It was too hot to continue pulling weeds, so she returned inside with Hal. Liz kept going to the front window all afternoon. She was sure the man was out there, waiting for her to come outside again.

The following day, Renz was almost like his old self. He ate his food and played with some of his toys. Liz and Hal spent much of the day with him, enjoying each moment, hopeful that the cancer treatments were working. The vets at the animal clinic where they took Renz twice a month were not encouraging. Nasal cancer was almost always fatal. However, there was a slight possibility that Renz would be the exception, so Liz and Hal did everything they could to help him survive.

Liz, still rattled by the man who had threatened her, continued to watch out the windows in case he returned, but he never did.

The day after, Renz was back to feeling feeble again. He refused to eat and drank only a small amount of water. He hardly moved from his position under a small end table, where he dozed or watched wearily as Liz or Hal moved about the room.

It was a long day. Liz kept hoping Renz would perk up again. She and Hal had felt so much hope yesterday. But Renz barely stirred.

As the sun began to set, Hal took Renz out so he could retire early that evening. Liz watched from inside the house as Renz walked around in the grass, looking up at the sky before lying down. Hal managed to get Renz on his feet again.

Hal opened the door and waited for Renz to follow him inside. Renz wobbled a bit as he walked over to his water bowl. He drank a small amount and then took a few steps to where Liz stood by the kitchen sink. Liz watched as the light faded from Renz's eyes. Renz began to kneel and then collapsed at Liz's feet, quietly passing through life's final roadblock.

The Story Behind the Story

This story is a fictional account of my dog Halo's last few days. Caring for a dying pet is very stressful, and when you have to deal with unpleasant circumstances on top of that, it is even more so. We face many roadblocks as we journey through life until we reach the final one and quietly pass through it. I often write stories based on actual events to examine my feelings within the safety net of fiction.

How to Fit in When you Don't

Long before I was a published author, I decided I would benefit by joining a writer's guild. I was living in Atlanta at the time. The Atlanta Writers Club sounded good. I would have lost my nerves if I had known how large its membership was and that Margaret Mitchell, the author of *Gone with the Wind*, belonged to the group when she was around. The club met on Saturday afternoon at the library. I was nervous about going since I wasn't a writer, just a dreamer. On my way to the meeting, I got lost and never made it to the meeting. What a relief that was.

The following month, I had this nagging feeling that I should attend the club meeting. As I walked into the library, my heart was pounding. When I sat down among all these writers talking about their work, I felt like an idiot. But then, one member turned to me and asked me what I had written. That's all it took. Before long, I sounded like one of them.

I quickly determined participating was the easiest way to fit into this group. I helped with club events, and although I had no experience, I agreed to facilitate a critique group. I think I was the one who learned the most from this experience.

When we moved to Knoxville, I again joined the Knoxville Writers Group. I felt more comfortable this time and eventually became the newsletter editor. I also facilitated another critique group.

Whatever your interest is, find a group that supports it and get involved. It's the only way you will ever fit in.

SÉANCE

It was a Friday night. Earlier in the week, the girls who lived on the fourth floor of Diane's dormitory had decided to hold a séance, and they wanted her to conduct it.

"Why me?" Diane had asked.

"You seem more mystical than the rest of us," said Carolyn Johnson. "You're always talking about ghosts you've seen, and more than once, you've told us that you could communicate with the dead."

"Well, I don't know if I ever talked to anyone on the other side. But okay, I'll do it."

The séance was scheduled to begin at eleven p.m. on Friday, October 13. The girls had decided to meet in Carolyn's room since her roommate was going away for the weekend. About fifteen girls planned to attend, so sitting space would be tight.

Linda Tompkins agreed to be Diane's assistant. Together, they planned the séance and decided on the props needed for the occasion.

"We have to have all the elements: earth, wind, water, and fire," stated Diane.

Before the event, Diane and Linda placed a cloth on a small wooden table. They then centered a candle on top of it, representing fire or light. A small bowl was set on either side of the candle, one with sand symbolizing earth and the other with water, which stood for rebirth and healing. The final element was wind, which couldn't be contained, so Diane and Linda opened a window to let air into the room, bringing knowledge and communication.

After Linda lit the candle, everyone grew quiet. She then turned off the ceiling light, leaving the girls in a shadowy semi-circle across from the table. Diane slowly scanned their faces before closing her eyes. When she opened them again, everyone stared intently at her as they waited for her to begin.

Diane held both her arms outstretched with her hands opened wide.

"Welcome," she announced. "The spirits are with us tonight and will reveal their message through me. I ask that you not speak unless requested and do not move about."

Diane placed her hands flat against the table as she gazed at the dark ceiling. She took a couple of breaths, then lowered her head and faced the group.

"I am receiving the number eighteen. Does that mean anything to any of you?"

"I'm eighteen years old," said Becky.

"That applies to almost everyone in this room," stated Diane.

Several of the girls laughed nervously.

"Does that mean we are all going to die?" asked Carolyn, who was somewhat superstitious.

"Nothing of the sort. Now, let's move on." Diane placed her hands back on the table. "Again, does the number eighteen mean anything to you?"

"My dorm room is number eighteen," volunteered Sarah.

"Okay, now we are getting somewhere. Do you have a male friend you very much care about?"

"I do; his name is Peter."

"Have you seen or heard from him lately?"

"No, I've been a little worried about him."

"Do you know where he is?"

"Not exactly. Peter went on a hiking trip to a foreign country a while back. I can't remember where it was. Do you think something has happened to him?"

"No, from all indications, he is doing well. He thinks about you a lot."

Diane was beginning to feel uncomfortable. There were no spirits, and she was making up everything she said. Still, she decided to continue with the séance.

"Does the letter G mean anything to any of you?"

"Peter's last name begins with G," Sarah quickly responded. "His last name is Gray."

"And did he drop out of college?" asked Diane, wondering where this thought came from.

"Yes, so he could go on the hiking trip."

"I see," said Diane, who had hoped to turn the attention to someone else. "Did Peter lose someone special recently?"

"His younger brother, about six months ago." Sarah was convinced that the spirits were trying to talk to her. Either there was something about Peter they wanted her to know, or they were using information about him to verify she was the one they wanted to communicate with during the séance.

Diane, on the other hand, wanted to end the session. Things had gotten out of control, and she didn't want Sarah to believe something that couldn't be proven. What if something terrible happened to Peter, now or later on? Diane would never forgive herself. At the same time, Diane wondered if perhaps she was receiving messages from the spirits. What if that was the case? Stopping the séance could prevent her from knowing information that might be important for Peter or Sarah.

A sudden breeze came through the open window, causing the candle to flicker spookily. There were a couple of gasps and some nervous shifting among those in the semi-circle.

"Everyone, listen," Diane said. "I think we should end the séance."

"Why?" asked one of the girls. "We're just getting started."

"Well, honestly, I thought this was mostly a joke. I've never conducted a séance before. I didn't even know what I was doing. But then, the messages started coming, so I kept going."

"We can't stop now," pleaded Carolyn.

The other girls nodded.

"But I'm scared. I don't want to do this." Diane stood up and hurriedly walked out of the room. Linda was close behind her.

"Where do you think you're going?" asked Linda.

"Out of here."

"Well, you need to go back and finish the job."

"But I feel like a phony. I don't have any magical traits."

"But everyone in that room thinks you do. Do you know how those girls would feel if they thought you made all this up?"

"The problem is, I don't know if it was made up. Maybe in the beginning, but then it seemed very real. Perhaps I am a psychic."

"Whatever you are, you need to go back and figure out a graceful way to bail out."

Diane and Linda walked back to the room. Two girls had left, while those remaining shared their disappointment in Diane's unwillingness to continue the session. When Diane sat back at the table, the others returned to the semi-circle.

"I ask the spirits to return, welcoming them to our circle so everyone in this room can receive their guidance. May all the participants remain safe and protected during this session."

Carolyn and Sarah glimpsed each other, wary of what to expect.

"If a message is intended for our friend Sarah, we implore that you make it known." Diane's stomach felt queasy as she wondered what had possessed her to continue the session.

No one made a sound. Then, suddenly, the candle blew out, leaving the room completely dark. There were a few short screams as Diane struggled to find a match to relight the candle. The wind outside had picked up a bit, and it was beginning to thunder. Diane lowered the window when it started to rain. She looked at her watch. It was almost midnight.

"Again, good spirits, is there a message you wish to deliver? If not, we will end our session and allow you to return from where you came."

The landline phone on the wall of the dorm hallway rang, breaking the silence and startling everyone. One of the girls got up and ran to answer it.

"It's for you," the girl nodded toward Sarah as she entered the room.

"For me? Why would anyone call me at this hour?"

"Well, answer it," Carolyn said.

"Hello," said Sarah. A few seconds later, the others heard her scream as she dropped the receiver that was now banging against the wall.

Linda put the receiver to her ear. A male on the other end repeated, "Sarah, Sarah, Sarah," several times in a slow, creepy voice. The music in the background was like a funeral dirge. Linda handed the phone to Diane so that she could listen in, too.

"Do you have any idea who the caller was?" Diane asked Sarah.

"Not at all."

"Well, someone must have known about the séance. The call has to be a prank."

Diane quickly ended the session and suggested no one talk about it the rest of the night. It was late; hopefully, the caller would not bother calling back.

What concerned Diane the most was that even if the phone call was a prank, how would the caller have known to target Sarah? Maybe one of the girls who left early set it up. But why would they unless perhaps they didn't realize how upsetting a call like that would be? There must be an explanation, but Diane couldn't think of one.

A few days after the séance, someone knocked on Diane's door.

"Hi, I'm Gloria Wilkins. I live in Mason Hall. Are you Diane?"

"Yes, is there something I can do for you?"

"I hope so," Gloria replied. "I heard about the séance you conducted and was wondering if you would agree to do a session in the Little Theatre—the one that's only used for small events. Everyone says it's haunted."

"I'm sorry, I can't. I'm not a medium; I only conducted the séance for fun. But it turned into something different than we had expected. I'm not sure I would want to experience it again."

Gloria left disappointed, but Diane breathed a sigh of relief. She would never again try to communicate with the unknown world. And Sarah would always wonder who or what, either a spirit or a prankster, had tried to summon her that night in a dorm room, but why?

The Story Behind the Story

This story will always remain a mystery. Was Diane able to make contact with the unknown, or did the girls at the séance believe what they wanted to believe? I had hoped that by sharing this experience, an answer would appear. If anything at all, it is more of a mystery than ever, especially for Sarah.

Life in a Box

When I began writing my novel *The Sand Rose*, I went through four large boxes of memorabilia, searching for a letter from my cousin Jay. Unknown to us, we were both in Saudi Arabia at the same time in the 1980s. Jay was in the U.S. Air Force, and I was on a temporary assignment. It wasn't until I was back in the States that I learned we were like "ships passing in the night."

While going through the boxes, many parts of my life leaped at me. There were people and events I had forgotten. There were letters from all around the world. Some of them made me sad. I suppose you might wonder why I saved so many old letters. The letters are a yardstick for measuring my growth—they say much about me at particular times.

There were other things, too, besides letters: Paul Mauriat's signature on a concert program (French composer of "Love is Blue" fame), a detailed analysis of my handwriting, songs I had written (words only), and examples of my calligraphy work. I found copies of projects I had worked on— such as designing the prototype for checks for Aramco in Saudi Arabia (I signed the prototype as "Alfred E. Newman" (from *MAD Magazine*). The list goes on and on.

I laughed and cried—but mostly, I felt grateful that I had preserved so much of my life in a box.

The Wandering Ramp

The day after the hail storm, Shelly went to the attic to look for roof leaks after seeing several wet spots on the second-floor ceiling. She had already called a roofer to come over to inspect the damage.

When the roofer arrived, Shelly led him to the second-floor storage room with an open staircase to the attic. There was only a tiny amount of light coming from a gable window. The light switch was on the other side of the attic, but Shelly had to climb over ductwork for the air conditioning unit to get to it. Although it was dark, she was familiar with the layout of the attic. Once Shelly had cleared the ductwork, she walked toward the switch. She felt the floor giving away as she stepped on the fold-down attic stairs, which opened to the second-floor hall below. Shelly struggled to hang onto the edge of the attic floor to keep from falling as the stairs unfolded beneath her.

The roofer rushed over and tried pulling Shelly up through the staircase. After his unsuccessful attempts, Shelly's adrenaline kicked in as she pushed herself upward to the attic floor. After lying down, she raised her upper body and saw her twisted ankle.

"I'm going to call an ambulance," the roofer said. "Are you in any pain?"

"No pain," said Shelly, "but you should probably go downstairs and get some ice or a bag of frozen vegetables to put on my ankle. I also need you to call my husband."

After informing Shelly's husband Gary about the accident, Shelly asked the roofer to go next door and get her neighbor Penny, a nurse, to come over. Penny came immediately, followed by a fire truck and an ambulance with six rescue crewmembers altogether a few minutes later. It was almost like a party in the attic when Gary arrived home.

Getting Shelly out of the attic wasn't going to be easy. The emergency crew decided the best way was to carry her down the open staircase on a backboard. They would then have to continue taking her down the winding staircase to the first floor. But first, they would have to pass the board with Shelly on it back and forth like a hot potato from one team to another over the ductwork.

"Whatever you do, Mrs. Greene, don't touch anything. Don't grab hold of the wall or the staircase railings; you've got to trust us. It's important not to lose balance, especially going down the stairs. Just close your eyes. We're going get you out of here."

Shelly breathed a sigh of relief once she was in the ambulance and on her way to the hospital. The orthopedic surgeon on call set Shelly's ankle after determining she had broken it in three places and then scheduled her surgery for the next day.

"You cannot put any weight on your foot," Dr. Wayne said when he checked on Shelly the day after her surgery. "You'll be in a wheelchair for a good while, and I don't advise you to use crutches."

Gary spent the next two days preparing for Shelly's hospital release. He arranged for a wheelchair and a hospital bed and then stocked food and other supplies. However, Gary hadn't figured out how to get Shelly inside the house since all three entrances had steps. On one of his trips to the garage, he spotted the dog ramp that their dog Charlie had used while his torn ligament was healing. One ramp would not work, so he bought a second ramp from the pet store. His plan wasn't ideal and possibly unsafe since the dog ramps were far shorter than the standard length for a wheelchair ramp. Gary decided to stick to his plan since the back door had only two steps.

Gary parked the car, unfolded the wheelchair, and helped Shelly transfer from the car to the chair. He opened the backyard gate and transported Shelly to the back porch.

"You can't be serious," Shelly said when she saw the makeshift ramp Gary had put together.

"Well, I don't know how else to get you inside. You're going to have to trust me, Shelly."

Pushing the wheelchair up the ramp proved more difficult than Gary had imagined. When it almost rolled back on him, Shelly gasped, fearful that her husband would end up flat on the pavement. Gary gave the chair a final push, landing Shelly inside their home.

"We need a better solution," said Shelly.

"I'll call those two carpenters who did some work for us a few weeks ago."

The carpenters could come over the next afternoon, and by the following day, they had completed a twelve-foot ramp made of pressure-treated lumber. On both sides of the ramp were railings made of 2 x 8-floor joists with a plywood overlay. And even though the ramp was quite sturdy, they bolted it to the concrete patio, ensuring it wouldn't move a speck.

Initially, the ramp was just a safe and convenient way for Gary to get Shelly in and out of the house. Later that week, Shelly's therapist showed her how to go up and down the ramp without assistance and lock or unlock the door. For Shelly, this was independence. She could now go outside with Charlie, and Gary would have less to complain about each time they had to go somewhere now that she could get to the car without his help.

Once Shelly's ankle had healed enough for her to walk, she and Gary started thinking about removing the ramp since it took up a lot of space on the patio and was too heavy and bulky to move without help.

"I thought of something," Shelly said. "Susan Gabriel could use a ramp since her cancer has worsened, and I heard she's now in a wheelchair."

"I don't know," said Gary. "We can't just pick it up and carry it to her. And besides, it was custom-made for our house, and the slope has to be just right."

"I've already spoken to some guys at Susan's church. They'd like to come by and look at the ramp."

After looking at the ramp, the three men determined it could be retrofitted to Susan's back deck. It would have to be disassembled and moved in a trailer owned by one of the guys.

The men took the ramp apart and transported it to Susan's house on Saturday morning. Shelly, Gary, and several other friends of Susan brought food and drinks for everyone. Dark, threatening clouds began to form as the guys worked furiously to reassemble the ramp, but fortunately, the severe thunderstorms predicted bypassed them altogether. When Susan made her triumphant ride down the ramp, a beautiful rainbow arched across the sky, bringing tears and applause to everyone there.

"You don't know how much this means to me," said Susan when she finally talked to Shelly.

"Oh, but I do," said Shelly. "I'm so glad the ramp did not have to be scrapped, and you will get much use from it."

Three months later, Susan passed away. Soon after, Susan's husband contacted Shelly about the ramp, more or less suggesting she could have it back. Fortunately, the guys who had done all the work disassembling the ramp and putting it back together again knew of an older man in a wheelchair who could only get in or out of his house if someone was around to assist him.

"I bet you never thought your ramp would end up serving others the way it has," said one of the guys to Shelly when he called to inform her that the ramp was about to go to a fourth person after the elderly man moved to an assisted living home and no longer needed it.

"I would have never thought such," said Shelly, "but I'm glad that's the case. Until I was in a wheelchair, I never knew the difficulties people with disabilities face. It makes a big difference if you have the means to maintain some of your independence."

Retro-fitting the ramp as needed for each person who needed it temporarily or for the rest of their lives had become a ministry for the men from Susan's church. Although modified multiple times, the quality of the materials used for the original construction assured the ramp's longevity. Once word got out about the project, it became known as the "wandering ramp" and served as an inspiration to all who knew its story.

The Story Behind the Story

This story is based on when I broke my ankle similarly a few years ago. Like in the story, the ramp made for me was passed on to at least four other people who needed one. I hope it is still making the rounds and helping others with temporary or permanent disabilities.

My Indian Summer

Most of the time, Indian Summer refers to an unusually warm, dry season in late autumn. Metaphorically, it can mean a renaissance of the heart, such as when something causes someone to feel young again. For me, Indian Summer has a more literal meaning.

It started with a knock on the door. My best friend at the time was house-sitting at her in-laws while they were out of town. Her father-in-law was the city's mayor and lived in a large home in one of the better neighborhoods. When she opened the door, Gail was greeted by three young men. They were from India and were attending graduate school in New York. During the summer, they were selling Bibles across the Southern Bible Belt. Ironically, most people in that region don't need another Bible, but these three weren't having any difficulties convincing them otherwise.

Gail began a friendly conversation with them, and before long, she invited them over to meet her friends, including me. Yogesh, who often wore a Western shirt; Kukie, a turban; and Joey, a silk cap were delightful. Our gang spent many evenings hanging out and getting to know each other. And we all shared the same trepidation when Joey almost drowned while swimming in the lake that summer. But I also remember some of the stares I got from small-town people when I once went to dinner with Yogesh. These people would call the police if they saw someone who didn't look like them sitting in the park and reading a book. I kept in contact with my Indian friends when they returned to school. I still have the letters they wrote me.

After Yogesh returned to India, I received a red wedding invitation for his marriage to his bride, Asha. The reception was held at the Taj Mahal Hotel in Bombay (now Mumbai). I wish I could have gone.

Nevertheless, it was a pleasant memory and taught me how much we can have in common with people from different cultures if we open the door and let them into our lives.

Turnipseed

JoAnne, Michelle, and Kelley lived in a three-bedroom house off campus, where their friends often gathered on evenings and weekends. Everyone, even strangers, was welcomed there.

One weekend, friends of the roommates, a couple from Alabama, visited overnight. Michelle offered them her bedroom since there was a couch she could sleep on in JoAnne's room, which was previously a closed-in porch and larger than the other two bedrooms. Shortly after the couple arrived that evening, they went to see other classmates they had known before Brad graduated last semester. He had recently joined the Army and was stationed on a base in Alabama.

"We won't be gone that long," said Fran as she and Brad walked out the door.

Around eleven o'clock, the roommates got tired of waiting for their guests to return and decided to go to bed. Before all the lights were off, they heard a knock on the door. All three girls assumed Fran and Brad had returned from their outing. When they opened the door, they were surprised to see a young man rather than their friends.

"Sorry to bother you this late at night. I'm Tim. I'm trying to catch a ride to Alabama. Some guys at a party told me I should check with you all."

"Oh, you must be friends of Fran and Brad," said Kelley. "They're leaving for Alabama sometime tomorrow. I guess you're riding back with them."

"I guess so," said Tim.

"What was your name, again?" asked JoAnne.

"Tim, but everyone calls me by my last name, Turnipseed."

"Are you kidding?" laughed Michelle.

"I've never heard that name before. Our friends should be back at any moment," said JoAnne. "You're welcome to sleep on the living room sofa. Knowing Fran and Brad, they will probably want to set out early in the morning."

Even though the girls felt safe, they wished their friends would hurry up and return. Turnipseed had already taken his shoes off and stretched out on the sofa. After making sure Kelley felt comfortable sleeping alone, JoAnne turned off the overhead light in the living room. Once in her bedroom, she secured the hook and eye latch on the bedroom door. Michelle took her place on the couch and covered up under a blanket. Everything seemed settled.

Not long after they had drifted to sleep, JoAnne and Michelle were awakened by a soft knock on the door.

"Let me in," said Kelley in a low voice.

JoAnne cautiously unlatched the door and let Kelley enter.

What's going on?' she asked.

"I woke up, and Turnipseed was standing by my bed. When I asked him what he was doing in my room, he said he was looking for the bathroom."

"Oh my gosh," said Michelle.

"I pointed to the hallway and waited for him to return to the living room after he came out of the bathroom, but he came back to my room instead."

"How creepy," said JoAnne. "Did Fran and Brad ever come back?"

"I don't know," said Kelley. "I didn't hear them if they did, but I'm not about to check since I'd have to go through the living room to find out."

"What did he do once in your room?" asked JoAnne.

"I told him to get out. I waited a bit before coming to your bedroom. I feared he would hear me, but he must have gone back to sleep."

"What are we going to do?" asked Michelle as the roommates huddled against the door, hoping they could prevent Turnipseed from forcing it open since the latch was not that secure.

"We could call the police," said Kelley.

"No, he might hear us and do something stupid," said JoAnne.

The girls jumped when Turnipseed rapped on the door.

"What's going on in there? Open the door and let me in."

"Go away and leave us alone," replied JoAnne.

"I'd rather be in there with you, but okay, I'll leave you alone now."

The trio felt their skins crawl as Turnipseed howled like a woof from the living room. He then laughed as loud as he could.

"Fran and Brad must not be here, or they would have heard him," said Michelle.

"Why don't we go out the side door?" asked Kelley, referencing the entrance that opened onto the patio.

"I think we're safer inside," said JoAnne. "He might come outside, too, and then we'd be like sitting ducks."

"We're already sitting ducks," said Kelley. "There must be something we can do."

"This guy's a maniac, or he's high on something. No telling what he might do," said Michelle.

Soon, Turnipseed began conversing with what sounded like an imaginary friend. Eventually, all he did was mutter and then laugh uncontrollably.

"What do you think he wants?" asked Kelley.

"Hopefully, all he wants is a ride to Alabama," said JoAnne. "He never said, though, that he knew Fran and Brad. It was only a coincidence he was headed in the same direction as them."

"He knows we're scared," said Michelle, "so maybe he's just messing with us."

"My parents always said I should never answer a door to strangers," Kelley said.

JoAnne and Michelle nodded in agreement.

Suddenly, Turnipseed pounded on the bedroom door, causing the girls to scream.

"I'm going to bust this door down if you don't let me in," he shouted.

Michelle and Joanne quickly shoved a small desk against the door to reinforce it. All three girls then pressed against the desk to strengthen their barrier.

Turnipseed returned to the sofa. Once, they heard him enter the kitchen, raising more concerns.

"What if he gets one of our knives?" asked Kelley.

"Ok, let's stop trying to figure out what he's going to do," Joanne pleaded. "So far, he simply seems to want to scare us. I'm not saying he wouldn't harm us, but let's not dwell on it. We need to stay alert and take action if necessary."

"Well, there's no way I can get any sleep tonight," said Kelley. "I wonder what happened to Fran and Brad. You don't think he did anything to them, do you?"

"No, I don't think he even knows who they are. We made some bad assumptions, and now we must deal with them."

"Then what's our plan?" asked Michelle.

"I think we should stay put for tonight," said JoAnne. "Fran and Brad left all their luggage in the front bedroom. They'll have to come back for it. When it's light outside, we will come out of here together. We can say something to make Turnipseed think help is coming, and he'd better leave."

"Like what?" asked Kelley.

"I don't know. Maybe we can act like we're on the phone and say one of our parents is almost here. Or that Fran and Brad will be back any second."

"That might work," said Kelley.

"But what if it doesn't?" asked Michelle.

For the rest of the night, one girl at a time took a thirty-minute nap while the other two stood guard. Other than occasionally laughing out loud, Turnipseed did not bother them again.

When morning broke, the girls shoved the desk out of the way and slowly opened the door. They walked past the living room, where Turnipseed was sprawled on the sofa. They began a conversation among themselves as they entered the kitchen, making sure it sounded like someone was arriving at any minute.

"They're almost here," said JoAnne. "We'd better get breakfast underway."

Michelle and Kelley pulled iron skillets out of the cupboards, intended as a weapon rather than a pan for frying bacon.

Turnipseed got up from the couch and poked his head in the kitchen doorway.

"How did everyone sleep?" he asked with a chuckle. "I look forward to meeting your parents."

"My dad will be furious if he finds out you slept here last night," said JoAnne. "You don't want to have a run-in with him."

"Okay, okay," said Turnipseed. "I get it. I'm leaving right now. You're going to learn someday," he finished with a scoff.

The girls ran to the front window to ensure Turnipseed had left for good. They watched until he was barely visible as he strolled down the road. After he disappeared, Fran and Brad drove up in front of the house.

"Sorry we didn't come back last night," Fran said as she exited the car. "Brad had too much to drink, so our friends insisted we stay with them. I didn't let you know because I didn't have your phone number."

"You all look like you've been up all night," said Brad. "Did we miss a party?"

"I wouldn't call it a party," said Kelley.

"Come on in," said JoAnne. "We'll tell you all about it. You don't know anyone named Tim—Tim Turnipseed, do you? He's from Alabama."

"I'd never forget a name like that." Brad chuckled.

"Neither will we," said Michelle. "Not ever."

The Story Behind the Story

This story is based on a similar event that took place when I was in college. It is a cautionary tale like the one by the Brothers Grim, "The Turnip," which reminds us of the unpredictability of life and the importance of being prepared for unexpected events. It is similar to the Geico commercial, where everyone hides behind the chainsaws instead of getting in the running car. We make bad decisions when we're afraid or feeling stressed. Our minds can become so twisted that we think our thoughts are rational.

Weeding and Writing

It's that time of year when I have to spend a certain number of hours and energy weeding my flower beds. I don't particularly like doing it, but the results make it worthwhile. As I was deadheading my rose bushes this morning, I saw similarities between weeding and writing. Weeding removes unwanted, inferior growth that often chokes our garden of all its glory. Pruning shapes, controls, and redirects the development of our plants, making them stronger and more appealing.

Writers are sometimes reluctant to weed out the words that may prevent their work from fully blooming. We often are too attached to words or phrases that interfere more than help tell our story. The best writing is kept simple. Just like my rose bushes this morning—there were so many spent buds that I couldn't see those starting to unfold.

Unwelcome Guests

It was an ordinary late afternoon in August, hot and humid, with only a light breeze to stir the air. Evening's quietness was beginning to settle in, even though the sun was still high above the horizon. Brad and Lindsey Collins sat talking, mainly about the littleness of their day, as afternoon slowly morphed into the evening.

"What are we having for dinner?" Brad asked. "It's almost seven."

"I'll get up in a minute." Lindsey was reluctant to move from her comfortable chair. Now that she no longer worked outside the home, her whims guided her schedule more than the clock. Dinner often got in the way of other things Lindsey was doing. Nevertheless, she liked being at home, even though she had never considered herself a housewife.

"We could go somewhere," Brad said.

"What was that?" Lindsey asked, turning her head toward the thump that had slid in between their conversation.

"What was what? Brad asked.

"That sound."

"I didn't hear anything," Brad replied.

Another thump. Lindsey was sure of it this time. Maybe a tree limb had fallen, or a careless bird had struck a window. Again, a thump, but more distinct, like a low knock.

"Someone's at the door. I'll get it." Brad got up and walked into the foyer.

Lindsey waited, wondering who would come unannounced at supper time. Then, she heard the door open, followed by an eerie guttural sound coming from the foyer. Lindsey straightened her back and cocked her head, straining to listen. The words were garbled, unlike any she had ever heard before. More than one voice, Lindsey determined. As she rushed toward the foyer to see who had interrupted their evening, she encountered two young men. They appeared as startled as she was.

What's going on here? Lindsey, bewildered, faced her unwelcome guests. They were no more than twenty years old, with eyes squinted and dark as night. Their thick black hair stood up in little spikes on top, their skin the color of a kraft envelope. Although their frames were slight and their stature short, the weapons they brandished made them powerful, menacing, and unpredictable.

Through the archway of the foyer, Lindsey spotted her husband lying on the stairway's landing. A third man held a 38 semi-automatic handgun to Brad's head. Lindsey's mind gyrated in all directions as she quickly assessed her situation. *Are these men here to rob us? I've got to keep calm. Let them take what they want. But why us, and in the light of day?* Her heart pounded like a racehorse at full gallop. The other two men blocked her path, frustrating her efforts to move closer to Brad.

Brad's body was as still as a corpse, other than the rise and fall of his chest. That, and the sound of his desperate breathing, was proof of life for Lindsey.

"Brad!" Lindsey called out to him.

Brad mumbled something in return, too low for Lindsey to hear.

"Shut up! Shut up!" repeated the man with a gun to Brad's head as he cocked the hammer.

Lindsey squeezed her eyes shut and stopped breathing. Nothing happened. She let out a sigh and opened her eyes again. One of the men moved closer to her, aiming the barrel of his handgun at her heart. His accomplice paced back and forth, nervously looking out the front room windows. *He's their lookout,* Lindsey surmised.

Lindsey stood with her feet cemented to the floor as her mind swirled in a strange universe that was half dream and half real. Her mind shifted between planning her escape and imagining a bullet burning through her chest. The sensation of swimming in her death was so intense she blacked out momentarily. Seconds later, she found herself fully conscious, with no memory of what, if anything, had happened during her lapse. Her instincts kicked in, and she began running for her life.

The man who had targeted her with his gun followed close behind. Lindsey could almost feel his breath against her skin as he uttered harsh, foreign words at her. He grabbed her arm just as she reached the back door. She jerked away and grasped the doorknob, turning it into what seemed like a slow-motion haze. Suddenly, the door was wide open. She could see the raised garage door of the house next door—her only sign of hope that someone might hear her desperate cry for help. But her long, high-pitched scream had no sound.

The man clutched her necklace as she scrambled to get out the door. She felt the gold chain dig into her neck as it separated and fell to the floor. Lindsey broke free again and almost reached the door before her pursuer grabbed her wrist and dragged her back into the family room where she and Brad had been sitting earlier. Now that she could no longer see Brad, Lindsey feared the worst had happened and she would be next. There was no time to think, no time to utter a prayer. *They're going to kill us,* her mind screamed as she prepared to die.

"Get down!" the man ordered, pointing his weapon to the floor.

I'm not getting on the floor, Lindsey vowed to herself as she struggled to figure out what the intruders intended to do with them.

"No," she said, wary of her voice.

"Get down!" he repeated with more urgency.

"No," she repeated, a little calmer this time as she searched his eyes for whatever mercy they held.

The man stared back at her with wide, astonished eyes as he took hold of one of her arms and pointed his pistol again at the floor.

"Take whatever you want," Lindsey asserted as she watched her fate unfold in her captor's eyes, "but get out of here."

The man shifted his gaze from Lindsey to something behind her. His pupils widened even more, and his mouth opened in surprise as he peered over her shoulder. Lindsey felt a chill go up and down her spine. She was too afraid to look at the unexplainable presence she had sensed behind her. She didn't move, blink, or even breathe.

Suddenly, the intruder released her arm and rushed toward the foyer. Only then did Lindsey turn around to see who was behind her, but no one was there.

A moment later, Lindsey heard the front door slam. The three invaders jumped into a waiting car driven by a fourth man as she looked out the front window.

Before she could catch her breath, she heard the door lock turning.

"Jesus Christ! Call the sheriff," Brad called out to her.

Thank God! Thank God! Overwhelmed with relief, Lindsey felt as though she might collapse. The page listing the significant numbers she had compiled that day for a women's club brochure was where she had left it, right next to the phone. She quickly spotted the number and called the sheriff.

"What is your emergency?" the voice on the other end asked.

"They've got guns! They've got guns!" Lindsey cried. She was in shock and unable to give the operator her name or address.

Brad rushed into the room. He took the phone from Lindsey as she sank to the floor in a pile of uncontrollable shaking and tears.

The sheriff arrived within a few minutes. He listened calmly as Brad and Lindsey shared the details of their ordeal, leaving them with the impression that what had happened in their home was commonplace.

"Mrs. Collins," the sheriff turned to Lindsey, "tell me again about the person you say was standing behind you after the other man ordered you to get on the floor."

"I don't know if it was a person," Lindsey responded.

"What do you mean by that?"

"I can't explain it," Lindsey said as she struggled to grasp what she had experienced.

"I can understand how scared you were. Probably, all kinds of things were running through your mind. The two of you are very lucky, you know."

"I know it sounds unbelievable," Brad said, "but what she told you is real enough for me. Haven't you ever had a gut feeling, Sheriff? Something you know, but you can't explain?"

"Most likely," said the sheriff, "you were the victims of a gang involved in numerous home invasions. I don't understand, though, what scared them off. Are you sure it wasn't one of them behind you, Mrs. Collins?"

"I'm sure," said Lindsey, still believing a guardian angel had saved them.

Brad and Lindsey looked at one another. The intruders had taken none of their belongings yet had robbed them of their most valuable possession—peace of mind. For them, their unexplainable escape from harm was no mystery.

Eventually, law enforcement rounded up a gang matching the description of the home invaders. Five men stood behind non-see-through glass in a lineup while Brad and Lindsey struggled to identify the men who had terrorized them.

"Were any of these men in your home?" asked one of the detectives.

"I can't be certain," said Lindsey. Brad nodded in agreement.

"Take your time," said the detective.

Lindsey carefully studied the faces of the men behind the glass.

"I am sure two of these men were never in our home," said Lindsey.

"Which two?" asked the detective.

"The second and fourth in the row."

"And you are a hundred percent sure of that? What about the other three men?"

"I can only confirm that the second and fourth men did not enter our home."

The disappointed detective thanked Brad and Lindsey for participating in the lineup. Then, as they left the police station a few minutes later, they were startled to see the two men they had ruled out walk past them. The two men were wearing police uniforms.

"Looks like you were right about them," said Brad.

"I'm pretty sure the other three men were the ones who held us captive, but I suppose we will never know. Why us, Brad? Why us?"

After that, every time the doorbell rang, Brad and Lindsey froze. They only opened the door if they were expecting someone or knew who was out there. Fear had made them prisoners, while their unwelcome guests remained free as birds.

The Story Behind the Story

This story is based on an invasion of my home many years ago. The fear of that event has never gone away. Nor has the mystery ever been resolved. Some speculate that the intruders intended to invade another house, not ours. We will never know. I wrote this fictional account to look at the circumstances more objectively. Yet, still, when the doorbell rings unexpectedly, it all comes back to me.

Learning to Love What is Wrong with Me

December 16 is often celebrated as Ludwig van Beethoven's birthday. But no one knows for sure what day he was born. We do know that he was Christened on December 17, 1770.

Almost everyone is familiar with his beloved composition *Moonlight Sonata*, which was completed in 1801—just as his hearing began fading rapidly. Eventually, he was totally deaf. Yet, he did not let that stand in his way. Although the memory of music remained with him, what allowed him to continue composing was his ability to audiate—which means to think musically or to hear music in his mind's ear, though no sound was present.

Having lost hearing in my left ear has made me rethink many things about my own life. At first, I was devastated about my loss, but lately, I find there are things to love about it. For one, if I sleep on my right side at night, I can enjoy almost total silence (other than the constant rush of wind in my ear). I can't hear Bob snoring or Kaspar "woofing" in his sleep. It's relatively peaceful. But strangely, I do often hear faint, beautiful music when my right ear is pressed against the pillow. When that happens, I turn over—thinking perhaps the radio alarm is on. But the music vanishes. I don't know where it's coming from. Possibly my memory of it. I am learning to enjoy these moments—real or imagined.

Even people with complete hearing do not hear sound in their dreams. It is imagined. In that way, people who were not born deaf but experienced hearing loss later on can also imagine sound.

Beethoven never stopped hearing the music in his heart. And that made all the difference.

Victoria Station

After her friends Brenda and Gary relocated to The Hague in the Netherlands, Cindy began saving the money she had made from working overtime on a special project to pay for a trip overseas to visit them. Cindy arrived in Holland on June 1, 1979. She slept most of the day in the small third-floor bedroom of her friend's charming but narrow apartment. By evening, she was wide awake, enjoying supper with Brenda, Gary, and two of their neighbors.

The next morning, Brenda and Cindy visited an open-air market. Later that afternoon, Gary drove them to Volendam, a lovely waterfront tourist town. For fun, they had their photos taken in traditional Holland costumes. Brenda and Cindy wore long skirts overlaid with a striped apron, white lace bonnets pointed on top, and wooden shoes. Although Gary laughed at them, they persuaded him to wear a traditional black jacket, baggy trousers with suspenders, and a thimble-shaped hat.

The trio took a ferry across the English Channel from Holland to England a day later. Before getting on the ferry, they found a shop that made *poffertjes*.

"What are these?" asked Cindy. "They're wonderful."

"Dutch mini-pancakes topped off with creamed butter, powdered sugar, and strawberries," said Brenda.

"The pancakes originated from Catholic tradition," said Gary. "They served as the sacramental host during the communion ceremony."

After enjoying their breakfast, they strolled around the area until it was time to board Gary's vehicle onto the ferry. After they parked, they went to the upper deck lounge for the seven-hour ride across the channel.

Once the friends reached England, they drove to Cambridge and spent the night. The city is home to one of the world's best universities, the University of Cambridge, which was founded in 1209.

"This is so lovely," said Cindy when she saw The Bridge of Sighs, a stone-covered bridge that crosses between River Cam and the campus of St. John's College.

"Supposedly, this bridge was Queen Victoria's favorite spot in all of Cambridge," said Brenda.

"I can see why," said Cindy. "Do you know when it was built?"

"Sometime in the early 1800s," Gary replied. "It was named after the famous bridge in Venice, but it doesn't resemble it."

The friends spent the rest of their time viewing several other colleges. Their favorites included Trinity College, founded in 1546 by King Henry VIII, and the King's College, founded in 1441 by King Henry VI.

"Where are we headed next?" asked Cindy as they got into the car.

"York," said Gary as he looked over his map.

When they arrived in York, they were greeted by folk dancers at York Minster, an Anglican Cathedral that dates back to the seventh century, performing the Morris Dance, which came to England in the fifteenth century. The dance blends tradition, mystery, and lively movements. Afterward, they went to Clifford's Tower, the keep of York Castle, built in the eleventh century as a fortified complex consisting mainly of castles, prisons, and law courts. By the nineteenth century, all that remained was Clifford's Tower.

"Let's get going," said Gary. "We can spend some time on Shambles Street before leaving York."

"I've heard of that," said Cindy. "Isn't it the oldest street in England?"

"It's the oldest street in Europe," said Brenda. "I love the winding avenues and overhanging buildings."

Eventually, they made their way to Northern England.

"This is like a fairy tale," said Cindy. "The winding roads, hillsides, and cottages are so picturesque. I hope the photos I've taken capture how lovely they are."

As they drove through a small village, Brenda suggested they stop and buy local bread, cheese, and apples. Next, Gary pulled off the road, close to a scenic view perfect for their picnic. It had been a long day, and it was now late afternoon. As they approached Scotland, they saw a lone man standing beside a welcome sign along the road. He was playing bagpipes and wearing a traditional Scottish kilt.

"I couldn't have asked for a better welcoming," said Cindy.

"I think we will wait until tomorrow to go sightseeing," said Gary. "Hopefully, we can find a place to eat near our hotel."

The next morning, they visited the Augustinian Jedburgh Abbey. The abbey is a mix of Norman and Early English architecture built in the twelfth century. They also came across Queen Mary's house. The Queen only lived in Jedburgh for a short time and is known to have said she should have died there rather than fleeing Scotland to seek protection from England. She was imprisoned for nineteen years before being executed.

Nothing was as grand as Edinburgh Castle, the friends agreed. Scotland's most visited attraction is perched on top of the rugged volcanic Castle Rock, which humans have occupied since the Iron Age. It was originally a stronghold where Scottish monarchs resided. There are several stairs or steps to reach Castle Rock's summit.

"I'm worn out," Cindy said as she and her friends left the castle.

As they walked around the city looking for a gift shop, an older woman approached them.

"Have you seen Bobby?" the woman asked.

"We don't know anyone named Bobby," said Gary.

"Greyfriars Bobby—oh, you must see him. Follow me."

Gary, Brenda, and Cindy looked at each other as they tried to figure out what the woman meant. But they were also curious and decided to follow her. Soon, the woman stopped and pointed to a statue of a Skye Terrier dog. Bobby had guarded his deceased owner's grave for fourteen years in the 1800s. A wealthy English woman who heard the story of the faithful dog commissioned a sculptor to create an image of Bobby.

"Thank you so much for sharing this with us," said Brenda.

"It was my pleasure." The woman clasped her hands and bowed slightly, then moved on to wherever she headed.

Over dinner that evening, Cindy announced that she would prefer to take a train to London rather than go with Gary and Brenda to Loch Ness. They could meet her on their way back from Scotland at Victoria Station. Cindy made reservations for the train and booked a hotel room across from the station.

In the middle of the night, Cindy woke up horrified that she had not signed the traveler's check she had given to a shopkeeper after purchasing several gifts for her parents and nieces. Since the shop wasn't too far from the train station, she left early enough to stop by and sign the check. The shopkeeper was so grateful that she insisted on giving Cindy a box of chocolates. Later, on the train, Cindy shared the candy with several people around her age whom she met on the trip to London.

"Oh my God," said Cindy as she stepped out of the train at Victoria Station. She was astounded by its size and wondered how Gary and Brenda would find her when they arrived in London. People were coming and going in every direction. She felt better once she was outside and walking toward her hotel. It was a small place, but it served breakfast.

The first three people she met upon checking into the hotel were Americans, two older women, and a young man whom Cindy guessed to be ten years younger than her.

"Does anyone know a good place to eat nearby?" asked the young man.

"No, but I would be happy to look for one with you," Cindy stated boldly.

Cindy and her new friend Roland spent the next few days wandering London's streets. They visited all it had to offer: St. Paul's Cathedral, Buckingham Palace, Westminster Abby, Big Ben, the Tower Bridge, Kensington Gardens, the Tower of London, and more. She was glad she came and, although concerned at first about traveling alone, everything had worked out in her favor. The only concern she had was how to find Gary and Brenda at Victoria Station the next day.

As planned, Cindy purchased matinée tickets to *The Mousetrap* for herself and her friends. The play had been running for over twenty-five years since its debut in 1952. Gary and Brenda drove to London, parked their car outside the city, then took a local train to Victoria Station.

When it was close to the established time for her friends to join her, Cindy made her way to the station, anxious that they might not find her. But she immediately spotted the large clock hanging from the ceiling in the station's center. Cindy decided to stand under the clock and let Gary and Brenda find her instead of walking all over the place hunting them. Her plan worked. Her friends saw her as they made their way through the crowds.

"Thank God you found me," said Cindy.

"We were a bit worried," said Brenda.

The trio enjoyed the performance that afternoon, followed by a light supper before taking the train back to where they had left the car. They spent the night nearby, and then the next morning, they took the ferry back to the Netherlands.

Cindy flew back to the States a few days later, taking many wonderful memories with her. But even in the short time she was away, an energy crisis had spread across the country, causing long gas lines and panic.

Cindy grew impatient as she waited to fill her tank, though she could do nothing about the inconvenience. The man behind her caught her attention in her rearview mirror. She determined he seemed distressed as he moved his head from side to side, looking for an escape route. He stretched his arm across the back of his seat and tapped his fingers impatiently. Suddenly, he jumped out of his car and ran over to her. Although startled by his rapping on her side window, Cindy rolled it down a few inches.

"I'm from England," the man said breathlessly. "I don't know what I'm doing."

"I just got back from England," shared Cindy, and the man calmed down a bit. "Don't worry. Stay behind me. After I fill my tank, I'll fill yours, too."

"Oh, you don't know what a relief this is," said the man. "I will never complain about the crowds in Victoria Station again."

Cindy smiled. She understood how stressful it could be to travel to another country. Her frustration over the long gas line disappeared as she gladly helped her fellow tourist.

The Story Behind the Story

This story is based on a trip to visit friends in the Netherlands. I can still feel the agony I endured over wondering if my friends would be able to find me in Victoria Station. Back then, no one had cell phones. If not for the big clock, we may have missed each other while wandering everywhere. As it turns out, people from all over the world use the clock as a meeting place.

The True Meaning of Life

Today, I was reflecting on what success was for me. For some people, success is centered around how much money they make, how much fame they achieve, how much they are loved or admired, raising a family, attaining spiritual enlightenment, conquering their weaknesses, and so on. It's different for everyone. But what I've come to realize is that true success is not something we will ever know. That may sound strange until you think about it in these terms: will we have made a difference for those who come behind us? Will we continue to influence lives positively? Will people look back on our lives and imitate us? As a writer, having my work endure is most important to me. Will it be read for generations to come? Will something I put on paper encourage others to live in hope and gratitude? I don't know the answer because I'm still here and still have much writing to do.

As I was thinking about this, I came across the following quote. I couldn't have said this any better than Scottish rugby player Nelson Henderson did in the late 1800s: "The true meaning of life is to plant trees under whose shade you do not expect to sit."

Patricia Taylor Wells published her first book in 2016: "Camp Tyler, A First of its Kind" for the benefit of Camp Tyler, the oldest outdoor education school in the country, which she attended as a child. Since then, Ms. Wells has published the following books: *The Eyes of the Doe*, 2017 (novel), *Mademoiselle Renoir à Paris*, 2018 (memoir), *LodeStar: Reflections of Light and Dark*, 2019 (poetry), *The Sand Rose*, 2021 (novel), *Kaleidoscope*, 2022 (poetry), and *Maple Point*, 2024 (memoir). Her awards include First Place for Family Life/Inspirational Fiction in the Best of Texas Book Awards in 2018 (*The Eyes of the Doe*), First Place for Poetry in the Best of Texas Book Awards in 2020 (*LodeStar: Reflections of Light and Dark*), and First Place for Poetry in the Indie Authors Awards in 2023 (*Kaleidoscope*). Since 2019, she has also received fourteen awards for short stories. Since 2016, *Tyler Today Magazine* has featured Ms. Wells eight times in its "Authors Among Us" column, which she helped inspire to benefit local authors. Ms. Wells, who holds a BA in English and French, facilitated writing critique groups for the Atlanta Writers Club and Knoxville Writers Group. She especially enjoys writing poetry and draws inspiration from the wide range of experiences she gathered from her travels and living in various places.

Please visit her website at www.patricia-taylor-wells.com